T0149387

Memories from the East

Memories from the East

Pearls & Tears

Abdulla Kazim

authorHOUSE®

AuthorHouse™
1663 Liberty Drive
Bloomington, IN 47403
www.authorhouse.com
Phone: 1-800-839-8640

© *2012 by Abdulla Kazim. All rights reserved.*

No part of this book may be reproduced, stored in a retrieval system, or transmitted by any means without the written permission of the author.

First published by AuthorHouse   01/05/2012

ISBN: 978-1-4678-8268-2 (sc)
ISBN: 978-1-4678-8269-9 (ebk)

Library of Congress Control Number: 2012900213

Printed in the United States of America

Any people depicted in stock imagery provided by Thinkstock are models, and such images are being used for illustrative purposes only.
Certain stock imagery © *Thinkstock.*

This book is printed on acid-free paper.

Because of the dynamic nature of the Internet, any web addresses or links contained in this book may have changed since publication and may no longer be valid. The views expressed in this work are solely those of the author and do not necessarily reflect the views of the publisher, and the publisher hereby disclaims any responsibility for them.

For the best flower of her country, Thuraya

1

I was six years old. I would turn seven in the coming June, which was just ten days away. I had a toy in my hand and many others in front of me on the ground, ten characters of Naruto anime. These were not all that I had; I had a cupboard full of toys. I liked to collect characters of the anime cartoons I used to watch. I remember having the full character set of Bleach, Death Note, Rorouni Kenshin, and One Piece.

My small black PSP was placed on the tiny white-framed aluminium chair, whose yellow-leathered oval seat and back rest were very comfortable. Just ten minutes ago I had been holding that PSP and playing the Street Fighters IV game. The device was my mother's gift to me for excellence in my studies the previous year.

I was busy making fantasies about the Naruto characters that were laying in front of me, with Naruto, the main character, in my hand. I fantasised about Naruto having a fight with his friend, Sasuke. As I remember, my fantasies about the battles between the characters and fight

1

scenarios were actually more dramatic and much closer to reality than what is shown in the anime cartoons.

I was quietly mouthing noises that would be actually the result of clashes between heroes on the television, but these noises were not loud enough to prevent my ears from catching the noise that came from the main door of the house. The sound was loud enough to startle me, silence my mouth from making noises, stress my nerves, and cause my eyes to fix on the door of my room, which was fully closed. That noise was caused by the main door slamming loudly. My heart jumped in my chest and I swallowed hard, as I recall.

But then I heard the coughing voice of my father, and my nerves relaxed. I went back to playing with my toy characters light-heartedly. The reason why that door-slamming noise frightened me for a while was that for the past week my father had been acting a little awkwardly towards my mother, and my mother seemed a little sad and always bad-tempered. I couldn't understand at the time what was happening, but I realized that something wrong was going on between them. The whole of the previous day, my mother hadn't come home. I asked my father about her, and he replied that her auntie was sick and thus Mother was needed to take care of her.

After a few seconds, I heard some more noises coming from the kitchen, and my thoughts went directly to Father making our lunch. The day before he had made a grilled chicken, which had come out half-burned. He laughed with me, but we ate together in the absence of my mother. I didn't mind these new noises either. I just felt comfortable hearing my father's coughing; it made me feel that I wasn't totally alone.

He had started that coughing attack the previous week, and he still had it. I knew that father didn't like being sick, and he hated coughing, but for me it was like some relaxing music. I had started observing some quarrelling between Father and Mother about three weeks earlier, and since then my mother had treated me badly; she would shout at me, say bad words to me that I didn't understand at the time, and would even slap me, the physical agony of which varied from one day to another. I think that was the time Father developed his coughing. He used to protect me always from my mother and all other oppressions in life. He was my guardian and my example.

I was playing in my room and waiting for my father to call me to come and eat with him, as he had done the day before. However, an hour passed since I first heard his coughing, but I did not receive any call from him.

I got bored making stories and scenarios with my toy characters. I collected my Naruto characters slowly and carefully; I always kept my toys in good shape and had never broken any of them. I was praised for that by my father and uncle—for being so tidy a kid and so thoughtful in dealing with the elements of life at such an early age. I opened my toy cupboard, which was divided into two levels. That cupboard was specially allocated for my toy characters; I had different stores for other types of toys. As I said, I was a very neat child. The neighbourhood children I knew used to like to play in my room. They could find the toy they were looking for very easily, but

I made strict rules for them: no toy may be broken, and every toy must be returned to its original location when done with. Just a few days earlier, I got very upset with a child who damaged my toy train. I sent him out my room and made a vow not to allow him in ever again.

I sat in front of the open cupboard and started arranging the Naruto characters, placing them in a good way and position. When I was done with this, I paused for a while to look at them, admiring the way I had arranged them. I turned my attention to other character sets in the cupboard. Luffy, from One Piece, was wearing his red sleeveless shirt, but his body had more muscles than were illustrated in the cartoon, and his shipmate, the green-haired Zorro, wore a harsh expression, holding a sword in each hand and one in his mouth. I enjoyed watching Zorro fight in the cartoon: a man holding three swords and using all of them perfectly—what a talent!

I closed the cupboard, went to my desk, and took out my drawing book and a pencil. I browsed through the first few pages of the book. All the pages held my drawings, and all of them were related to cartoon characters. Some were already coloured, while others were not. I sat down on the rugged floor and opened it to a new page. I recall getting that feeling of having missed seeing Mother and Father together and going with them to the fun city. I started drawing, almost unconsciously, two characters standing next to each other and looking at each other with smiles on their faces. Next to them stood a child with a popcorn box in his hand, with a smile on his face as well. When I was done with the characters, I started working on the background—all the different games available in the fun city. The characters on the paper might have looked like anybody in particular, but for me they represented my parents and me.

All the time I was working on my drawing, which took me about an hour, I could hear noises coming from the kitchen. They were the noises of a knife cutting through meat, as I guessed, because I used to hear my mother making those noises while cooking. I smiled to myself, recalling the grilled chicken pieces Father made the day before; they were very tasty. I hoped that he would serve the same dish again.

I recalled the day before when I had sat with him, just the two of us, father and son, at the table for lunch. I could see glimpses of concealed sadness on his face, although they were concealed by the small happiness of being with his only beloved son. I had always enjoyed talking with father; I just really did. I never sensed any boundaries between me and him, even though I was so young. Between me and my mother there were still boundaries in everything—talking, behaving, and playing. That day Father had told me a story, while I was chewing a piece of chicken in my mouth. He told me a story of a man who lost his heart in a battle and died shortly afterwards, not because he was left with no heart, but because he felt himself inhuman and greatly different from others around him. He was eaten up by his own sorrow. Father might have told this story on purpose, but it was of no interest for me. I continued eating as if I heard nothing.

And then it came finally, my father's call. Pleasure filled my heart, and I recall myself smiling. I closed the drawing book and placed the pencil on top of it. My father's voice came again, calling my name. I ran, opened the door of my room, and rushed out. I stopped running and started walking fast. My mother had warned me many times before not to run at home, as I might injure myself by falling on the floor or hitting any of the statues located in most of the corners of the house. But as I walked, my nostrils recognized a strange smell, but I couldn't name it exactly at that moment. My mind was busy thinking of the food prepared in the kitchen.

I stood at the kitchen door, and my heart fell heavily to my toes. I couldn't breathe and I didn't dare to breathe. Father was holding a butcher's knife in his hand that was fully dyed red.

"Come in," father said in a calm shaky voice. He followed that with the usual small cough.

Father had never tried to scare me with his tone—never before—but at that moment he put a hell of a fear in my heart. I stepped into the kitchen, not because I wanted to, but because of the heightened fear and confusion raging inside me.

"Come in," father said again, and then he lifted his eyes to the ceiling for a while.

My mind was totally lost in the scene, and a new set of voices started echoing in my ears. I could distinguish now the smell I had sniffed while walking to the kitchen. The smell was of blood, fresh blood. The echoing noises became louder and louder, little by little. I dragged my shaking legs and stood in the corner of the kitchen. Father had covered the kitchen's paint in red; he had made it rain in blood.

My eyes fell, and only then could they glimpse the shape of a corpse lying on top of the table. The long slightly brown hair brought to my mind the image of a particular person. In shock, the name of my mother, Huan, echoed in my ears. All of a sudden, the weight of my body was more than my legs could handle, although I always had strong legs and was the best athlete in my class. With my eyes dizzy, I reached back at the wall for support, but suddenly my body betrayed me, and I fell to the ground. I was even more frightened to think that there was something wrong with my body. My eyes were fixed on the hair of the corpse on the table.

"Gerald." Father's voice came to rock me once again.

I raised my eyes to look at him. I remember seeing his light-brown thick beard slightly touched by the redness that covered most of his body. Father was never good at chopping meat, and if mother didn't prepare something at home, he would most of the times make us of the ready-made food that would only require frying. Father pulled now something from the corpse and held it tightly in his hand. He raised that hand towards me.

"Look, Gerald," he said. "Open your eyes."

My eyes unconsciously turned to his raised hand. He was carrying an organ, which I was later informed was the heart. The organ was dripping blood on the floor, and that noise hugely alarmed me.

"This is the heart of women," father went on. "There is nothing in it. No love. No appreciation. Only greed and lust." He tightly clenched his teeth on the word "lust".

It was the first time I had seen my father express his anger in that matter. Then, all of a sudden, I heard a huge knock on the main door of our home. Father lowered his hand, which was holding the organ. He looked me in the eyes, and I could see now the same sadness in them that I had seen the day before. His eyes sparkled a little as well, which I later realized was caused by fighting back his tears.

The main door was knocked in with an exploding crack. The noise of a large number of thick-shoed feet came from behind me, and suddenly I saw about ten policemen standing at the kitchen door and in front of me. Sirens were sounding loudly outside in the street, which brought a couple of neighbours out of their homes. A bunch of guns were pointed at my father's face, and one policeman kept shouting at him in Chinese, ordering him to surrender and raise his hands. Father stood there still; he had surrendered already, before even calling the police, but he refused to raise his hands. A police man approached him, pushed him back, punched him in the stomach, and then handcuffed him, but father did not release a single sound of agony.

Suddenly, I felt a hand rise in front of me before and covering my open eyes. "Everything is going to be all right. You are safe," a voice said. I was held tight and snatched away from that terrifying scene. The idea of taking me away from that scene was a noble idea, but what I had already seen was more than enough for a sensitive child of my age to have witnessed.

2

$\mathcal{F}$ather was tried and found guilty. He didn't deny any of the charges against him, although the accusation that he was planning to kill me as well was far from the truth. I absolutely believed that my father would never hurt me physically in any way, and I still believe it. Father refused to talk to anybody during his short period of imprisonment; he even refused to get a lawyer. By doing so, father gave up his right to live and surrendered completely to the fate of death in a country where death is very frequent in the name of the government. Father refused to see me as well. All the years of love I had enjoyed came to an end at that point.

My ancestors on my father's side are originally from Russia. My grandfather was an activist and a writer in Moscow. After receiving many threats, he fled with his life intact to the United States. Within two months there, he found in that new county what he could not find in his own: a good job as a literature teacher in a decent university, respect from the people around him, freedom to write with an open heart, and above all a love that he couldn't find anywhere else. He got married soon afterwards, and the result was two boys: Leo and Eugene Arsov. Leo was my father. My father was named Leo because of the great passion my grandfather held for the great Russian writer Leo Tolstoy. Uncle Eugene was a year younger.

My father and uncle lived in the United States and never ever planned to return for any reason to the country of their origin. Father even hated Russia and called it "iced glass with hollow heart".

Leo and Eugene led a simple life in the United States, the country that welcomed them with an open heart. Uncle Eugene got married at the age of twenty to Elizabeth, who also originated from Russia. She is the sort of lady that brings true happiness to a husband's life. Uncle started a small hardware business in North Carolina with his wife. Father, on the other hand, liked to live a free life; he liked to know a lot of people and to try many different professions. At one time he started to work as a dancer in a night club, and he even worked for more than a month as a striptease dancer. He used to play tennis a lot, and my uncle thought he would be a professional player one day.

But father didn't find the lady he desired in the United States; he always had this vision of finding a beautiful Asian girl.

It was one Sunday when, after leaving church with his brother, father informed my uncle that he was leaving that very day and heading to China, without any given details. And he carried out that deed, in less than twenty-four hours he was in Beijing. Upon reaching a hotel, Father wrote to my uncle explaining the reason of the journey to the Far East: to meet the girl, he once got the number of from a friend, and to pursue love's trail.

Huan ("happiness" in English) is the name of my mother. She used to work in a perfume and skincare shop in the Beijing Capital International Airport. Father knew nothing about her other than what she told him about herself when chatting with him. In her conversations, mother expressed her feelings to my father. Father was not so certain about those feelings, but what encouraged him to consider them was the marriage of his close friend Paul Norman to a Chinese girl he met in a restaurant in Virginia.

Father wished to make his journey to China a surprise for Huan. Upon reaching the Beijing airport, he looked for the perfume shop. When he found it, he went in and strolled around slowly, looking for the face he wished to see in reality. When he saw her, he walked up to her and, to the surprise of all the staff there, he hugged her from behind and kissed her on the side of her neck. Soon the staff were whistling and applauding. Father asked my mother for marriage at that exact moment.

They got married within a month in China, and father started his new life there. He stopped being the careless person he used to be and gave up his curiosity about trying different professions for the sake of starting a family life. He became a quiet person. He took a job as a software programmer in a small private company. There he learned techniques of game programming, and I recall him sitting for hours in front of his computer working on lines and lines of code that seemed alien to me at the time. I still to this day keep some of his programs.

The married life of my parents continued smoothly till after my birth, but then the secrets my mother had sealed started to crack little by little, revealing her past lifestyle, her shameful affairs even while she was chatting with Father, and the lies about almost everything she had told him about herself. Father just accepted all this and wished to move on with his life with her and his son, me. And they did move on with their family life, but the month prior to the crime, Father was informed of Mother's affair with a police officer. It turned out to be true, but still Father wished to save the marriage for the sake of his love for her and for the sake of the innocent life of their son. That affair ended as a result of a small quarrel between my parents, only for mother to start a new affair with a mysterious guy. Nothing worked well, and father lost it all upon mother's declaration that she was planning to move away with that new guy.

That's when the crime came into the picture.

3

$\mathcal{N}$ow an orphan, I was taken on a journey to the United States, where Uncle Eugene was eagerly waiting for me. I recall that I shed a river of tears when I saw him and he took me in his arms. He welcomed me into his family and gave me the real kindness and tenderness that had been given to me previously by only one of my parents, my father. His wife Elizabeth was so good to me, and I became the son that she could never have. I loved her and respected her more than I had ever loved and respected my real mother.

The day after my arrival, my uncle and his wife accompanied me to the family psychologist. Uncle believed this was very necessary for the healing of my wounded soul; he strongly believed in finding a remedy for whatever disease one suffered from—in heart, soul, or physical body. But my poor uncle couldn't find the right remedy for his wife's inability to make a baby for him.

The psychologist consulted with me and held sessions with me for about a week. He spoke to me at the level appropriate for my age, and I still recall most of his lectures. However, he just couldn't grasp what I had been through. Uncle Eugene didn't get it, and Mother Elizabeth (if I have the right to call her so) didn't either. I acted dumb in front of the poor psychologist, and he did believe that I was carrying no pain in my heart whatsoever about watching my mother covered in her own blood, with her chest ripped open and her heart in the fist of my father.

How could I forget such a hideous scene? How could I forgive the loss of my parents? How could one forget and erase from his memory what was engraved in blood?

Uncle Eugene and Elizabeth, the most loving couple I have encountered in my life, have been cheated of finding the magic balm for my wounded soul, but they didn't know that the poison was in the wound, and the wound remained ever open.

Father didn't ever hurt me, but the wound he left in my heart the last day I saw him went very deep and opened all the doors of hatred within me.

4

My interest in toys ended at this time. Uncle Eugene bought me toys from time to time, but they only lay in my room, untouched and intact. I stopped watching anime cartoons, and I stopped caring about cartoon characters. I didn't even know what happened to my character collection back in China, nor did I care to know. That passion for toys was dead in me forever.

Instead I focused more on reading, writing, and thinking. After I turned seven, I started having different sorts of thoughts about death. I used to sit with my uncle and watch the news on the television. I would hear about a suicide bomber over and over. The word "suicide" bothered me at the beginning. While studying one evening in my room, that word became stuck in my mind. Out of curiosity, I went to the PC and searched for the word. I was surprised to learn that suicide is not always about hurting others around you; it can be limited to hurting one's own self. Afterwards, that word never left my mind for more than a week at a time.

Uncle sent me to schools, and some weekends he brought in a tutor at home to help me use my time. My passion for roaming around with others no longer existed; my entire focus started to fall on my inner sight—what I could feel rather than what I could see with my physical eyes. I didn't have any close friends at school, and Uncle could see that I didn't like it to mingle in with other lads. That was the reason why he started bringing in tutors at weekends.

After my twelfth birthday, I began to hear comments from the girls at school about my physical appearance—that I was handsome and cute. I was always whistled at admiringly by girls, even those older than me and in a higher grade. Some started calling me "Prince Charming". I didn't see myself a special boy then, nor do I see myself a special man now. I acted normal even on the occasion when a girl ran towards me and planted a quick kiss on my cheek. I was walking back to my class at the time after the break, and all the students in the yard started staring at me as if I had done something wrong. That girl was Fang Zhang.

Fang was a new girl in my school at the time, as I found out later, and she joined my class. She and her parents were also new to the United States. Her father got a job in the engineering field, and her mother worked as an aroma therapist.

I didn't deny the soft effect of Fang's kiss, and I did not avoid thinking of it, but I didn't wish to show its effect. Among all the girls, Fang was the only one who pushed herself towards me in an innocent way, without imposing herself on me. Others would send me dirty notes or brush their bodies against mine. Gradually, I began to feel a little closer to her. By the age of thirteen, I held her hand for the first time. By fourteen, I invited her to my home. Uncle Eugene and Elizabeth were very happy for the slight positive change in me. They knew Fang to be a good girl, and she truly was a good girl. But I wasn't a good boy.

Fang got to know about my passion for reading, painting, and writing and my curiosity to learn and try new things. She kept telling me, as did my uncle and his wife, that one day I would become a special person. They were correct about my many interests, but I couldn't understand what they meant by becoming a special person.

By the age of fifteen, I attempted to kiss Fang, but I couldn't. What prevented me was the image of my father saying, "This is the heart of women" with his blood-dripping fist.

If kissing a lovely girl is a pleasure, then that pleasure was denied to me by the thought of death. The image of death accompanied me always and stood as an obstacle that prevented me enjoying real life. I had lost some essence of my humanity. I couldn't understand any of the things rolling inside my heart, but I could vividly see my depression.

There is no point in living if what you see and feel is death. It is true that I had my many interests and my passion for doing things and learning things, but none of those put an end to me thinking and dreaming of death and the gravity of my depression. As I was about to celebrate my eighteenth birthday, I had made a vow—not to God, as I didn't believe in God. I had made a vow to myself that by the age of twenty-nine I would kill myself, commit suicide.

5

By the age of eighteen, I started publishing short stories. This started with school publications. I was one among the few at the school to publish short stories in the monthly magazine published by the school. My writings were always shadowed with pessimism and death. I wrote about love that was followed by betrayal, about peace that broke into war and ruin, about brotherhood that was accompanied by jealousy and envy, and about life that was curtailed by death. On one occasion the school editor called me to his office.

"You are such a good writer, Gerald," he started.

I looked at his face to read his expression; I saw lines of nervousness.

"I do expect a good future for you as a writer," he continued over his thick dark moustache. "But why do you write in such a dark way? Do you . . . understand what I mean?"

I nodded, and my eyes were still calmly focused on his face expressions. I could read what he was saying and what he was asking of me.

"Will you consider it for my sake?" he asked in a friendly way.

I nodded.

He shook my hand then, and we separated. What he was asking of me was to write in a brighter way—about love that ends in love, about peace that spreads all over the world, about life that ends in life, about things I couldn't see as true. He was trying to kill my creativity with rules that I couldn't see I should follow. I didn't stop writing, and yet I didn't see myself obliged to abide by the school's rules for publishing. For the next month's publication, I wrote another short story about killing ambitions. The story wasn't published, and the school refused to accept any of my stories any more. I didn't care about it—and I didn't even give a shit!

I was a good athlete. I liked gymnastics, running, playing football, and tennis. I brought home several medals in competitions involving my school and even in national competitions. Uncle was very proud of me. Elizabeth was very proud of me. Fang attended all the competitions I participated in; she didn't require or even ask for any invitation. I just concealed the feeling of comfort that seeing her brought me.

I participated with my classmates and schoolmates in some plays, such as *A Woman of No Importance* and *An Ideal Husband* by Oscar Wilde and *Macbeth* by Shakespeare. Elizabeth spent a lot of time with me rehearsing those plays. Everyone who watched the plays commended my acting, and many said that among all the others I was the best person characterizing his role. Although all this talk drew a big smile on the faces of my uncle and his wife, it failed to produce even the tiniest feeling of pride in me.

My hands were very delicate for drawing, and it just came to me naturally. While my other classmates were attending special classes to improve their drawing skills, I was better than most of them because I had perseverance and a stronger will. I was asked by a local children's magazine to join them temporarily in a project involving creating a new creative set of characters. I did so, and I learned new skills there. Later, I started making my own comics; I invented some characters and scenarios for their stories. I used to send them, with my signature, to some of my classmates, including Fang of course.

My art teacher kept asking me to join in art competitions and kept repeating his old-fashioned words of encouragement. I refused at the beginning because I was busy at the time learning to play the violin, but when he persisted, I finally agreed. Out of three competitions I participated in, we won two. My uncle asked me to get back the garden picture I had drawn for the second competition, in which we lost. I went to the room of my art teacher and there it was; the picture was hanging on the wall just behind his desk, but underneath was signed his name. How filthy he was and how low-spirited, that stupid teacher! I wrote him an angry letter upon my graduation. He tried to reach me several times on my mobile phone, but I didn't reply.

All my other interests did not affect my excellence in my studies. My grade sheet always carried A and A+ grades; I had never seen B in my school days nor in college. Elizabeth, my beloved mother, allocated one section at home for my medals, trophies, and certificates.

She and Uncle were more proud of me than I was myself. They just enjoyed looking at my extraordinary results in every field I attempted. They enjoyed talking of me to others—neighbours, friends, and guests. I was their son.

Everybody looked at me as a genius, something I didn't welcome very wholeheartedly. People always look at the output and ignore the details lying beneath. People ignore much and live with a low-spirited will towards achieving something, either because they are not running after any sort of achievement even at the personal level, or because they think that they still have a long life ahead of them. If today is missed, there is tomorrow, and thus days pass without being counted. But this was not the case with me. I had the desire to try out things of interest since no life was awaiting me after of my twenty-ninth year. So, whatever desire I might have, I had to fulfil it within the time limit of time I had placed on myself and my life.

I am no genius, you see. I am just someone who tried to satisfy his lust before meeting his planned destiny. If whatever I achieved—if it was to be called achievement—brought a little happiness to the beautiful hearts of Uncle Eugene and Elizabeth, then I am just glad.

The reader might ask why I didn't just discard the idea of suicide and live a normal life like any normal person. The answer is that you can pour the most tantalizing wine in the mouth of a dead man, but he still remains dead. We don't feel much once half our soul is already out of our body. I did try to step into life, but I failed. Since the day my father put me outside the gates of life, the gates remained locked in my face.

6

$\mathcal{F}$ang Zhang kept following me like my shadow. I didn't know really what she wanted of me. Sometimes she stood like thorns in my way. I did like the physical looks of girls, and I loved feasting my eyes with the sight of slender fit girls. There were many cute girls in my class and at school who admired me, or just my physical properties, but I couldn't have my way with any of them because of Fang. Everybody started to think that Fang was my girlfriend just because she was close to me always. What made it worse was the rumour Fang started distributing that we had made love a few times. I don't know why, but her words seemed to be believed without question. She hindered the satisfaction of my lust.

At the age of seventeen I joined some of the girls at school in arranging a craft and origami festival. I got this interest in handmade things when Fang invited me one day to just stand and watch her and her girlfriends work on some stitching, card designs, handmade necklaces and earrings, and gift-wrap boxes. I was really taken by the works they produced. Soon enough, I started mastering many of the things I had seen the girls work on. Fang was very surprised when I showed her some of my handmade gift-wrap boxes and origami flowers. She asked me to join her and her friends in the school handmade festival. I did so and enjoyed the experience.

At the time of the festival, we used to stay at school till four in the afternoon. Since I was the only boy among ten girls, I was asked, especially by Fang, to use the girls' washroom instead of walking all the way to the boys' washroom. Six of the other nine girls, excluding Fang, were really hot. I used to enjoy watching them slyly adjusting their clothes and bending over to pick up their stuff.

Uncle asked me to bring in Fang home for a visit after the last day of the festival. I didn't like the idea, but I couldn't come up with any objection. I obeyed his suggestion, and Fang was extremely glad to receive the invitation. I think that she thought it was more than an invitation from my uncle; she took it as an invitation from me.

Thus, at the end of the festival, the girls started going home one by one. Fang was standing by my side, but when I had finished cleaning the tables, I couldn't find her. My mobile phone rang; my uncle was waiting for us outside the gate in his Volvo XC90. I couldn't find Fang anywhere, but when I walked into the washroom, I realized she was there because of the sound of the locker. I stepped in and I could see her. She was naked except for the thin pink panties she had on. I could see the split of her ass and its shape with the panties slightly absorbed in. The image liquefied the solid water in my throat. She turned at me, and now I could see her hand holding her rainbow-coloured bra.

"Uncle is outside waiting for us," I said in as calm a voice as possible.

"I will be done in a minute. I was just taking a quick shower," she said.

I walked out and stood a few steps away from the door.

"Let's go." Her sweet voice came from behind me.

Before I had the time to even turn to her, she walked past me. She had on a knee-length brown linen flared skirt and a simple black tank top. At home, Elizabeth prepared us lunch. After lunch, there was homemade cake and cookies and tea. Elizabeth talked a lot with Fang, but I kept silent most of the time except when I was asked a question. My eyes fell on Fang's chest and legs; I recalled seeing her naked. I enjoyed recalling it, but it was stiffening my nerves.

Elizabeth asked Fang to spend the night with us, and Fang said that it was fine with her since tomorrow was Saturday, but she said she would ask her parents first. She picked up her mobile phone and walked outside as she dialled some number. I turned to Elizabeth.

"Why?" I whispered.

"Because she is a good girl. There is no harm, is there?" Elizabeth said with a smile. "We have a separate room for her."

Fang returned in a minute to say that her parents had no objection. I could see the happiness on her face as she said that. I just wanted to be away from her at that moment.

Dinner time came, and Fang helped Elizabeth prepare the meal. I was watching television, when my uncle sat next to me. He asked me about my ambitions in life. I answered frankly that I didn't exactly know. I was just a couple of months away from finishing my high school, and my uncle wanted me to choose a major of interest so that he could help me search for a proper college.

To be honest, I frequently had a dream of visiting China. I couldn't explain it to myself, but I could hear my heart requesting me to arrange a journey to the East.

"I might like it to go abroad," I said, without turning to uncle.

"That's good. Where to?"

"China," I said, and then, drawing a fake smile on my face, I turned to him. "I would like to study programming."

"I am happy hearing this from you, son. We will discuss it with Elizabeth." He paused for a while. "You know . . . your . . . was a . . ."

At this point Mother's voice came, telling us that dinner was ready. It saved me from hearing what Uncle was trying to say. I knew that he was trying to say that my father was a programmer. I knew it, but I just didn't like hearing anything about Father.

After dinner mother showed Fang one of the two guest rooms, and the room she told her to take was the one across from mine. After a while, as uncle went to his room and mother started washing the dishes, I retired to my room. I picked up a new book I had bought three days before, *War and Peace*, and started reading.

About an hour later, I heard a creak. I put the book down as I saw Fang standing at my door, and I smiled at her. She returned a sweet smile. She had on a pale pink nightdress, which perfectly complemented her creamy-white skin.

"Did I disturb you?" she asked.

I shook my head.

She slowly came in and closed the door behind her. Her eyes started roaming in the room.

"You've got so many interests in life." She picked up a yellow origami dragon from my desk. "Do you ever get bored with your life?" The question was alien to hear.

"Yes," I replied frankly. "I may even commit suicide one day."

She giggled, taking my words as a joke. My eyes kept exploring her from the top of my bed; she was so hot, so sexily slim. I could see her nipples, which suggested she was wearing no bra beneath the one-part dress she had on. My mind raised a secret question whether she was wearing her panties. My eyes were focused on her bottom. Despite the pale-coloured dress, I couldn't see her genitals.

All of a sudden, she approached and put her face in front of mine. Her silky black hair was tickling my face, and I could smell Nivea cream from her face.

"Did you like what you saw today?" she whispered.

She smelled so good! The fragrance of her mouth was a mixture of the mint toothpaste she used and her original sweet fragrance. It made me gasp inside. I got a hint of where her words were leading, but I wasn't sure.

"What?" I asked.

She reached her hand and placed it on top of mine. Then she seized my hand and with a slight force of her slim power, she pulled my hand and slipped it into her v-shaped neckline, then moving it and ending the journey on the top of her left breast.

I could see that what I had thought she was hinting was true. Her glossy body was under my control. I could see it vividly. Her long black hair fell like curtains on both sides of my head as she moved her body on top of me. Her face was still so close to mine that if I moved it a few inches towards hers, our noses would touch. Suddenly, small kisses were raining all over my mouth. My senses were stimulated, and I knew that I was losing it—losing myself to the moment. I brushed my free hand over her thigh, moving it slyly up under her dress and up again to her bare back. Her skin started getting moist and more delicious when my mouth returned her kisses. Her body pressed more against mine, and I added to its intensity with my hand on her back. I brushed my thumb on her breast, and with this motion, her wet tongue started brushing under my lips.

Despite everything I had achieved up to that time, I had never felt so close to heaven as at that moment. It was like heaven kissing the earth. It was like a gentle dream I didn't wish to wake up from. It was like reviving to life once again from the depths of my grave. It was like watching the twilight with your real eyes open and your emotions full of love. It was like finding yourself after being lost.

"This is the heart of women." My father's voice came to my ears, and I could see him standing in front of me holding the heart of my mother. I was so scared that my body started shivering. I opened my eyes and held Fang very tightly in my arms. I had a gasping attack. I could hear Fang's voice, troubled and frightened, asking me about what was going on with me.

"It is fine . . . it is . . . fine," I said, calming her down. "Please go to your room . . . I cannot do it . . . I am sorry."

Fang stood on her feet and stared at me wearily for a while before going out the room. I didn't feel sorry for hurting her in any way. I didn't feel sorry for disappointing her, and I had no plan to give her any explanation. I had no feeling at the time but that of anger. The memory my father had given me was so intertwined with my heart and mind. It broke down my moments of paradise.

7

The pure feelings Fang aroused in me that night had befriended me and accompanied me ever since. My thoughts were disturbed, and my ideas were shattered here and there, so that I found it hard to collect myself altogether without thinking, even for a split second, about her ivory body and rosy scent. It haunted me day and night, and even Elizabeth noticed something different in my expression.

But none of this stood as an obstacle in the path of my desire to finish my studies. The king inside of me, however inferior, refused to give in to the filthy rugs of my whims. I had finished my high school successfully and was the top of my class and the tenth in the whole state.

I was packing my clothes for the journey to China when Elizabeth came to me to say that Fang was on the line. I didn't believe this girl. Although I had ignored her since that night, she hadn't given up on me. Despite what was said about my physical beauty, I strongly believed that she could find better-looking boyfriends than me. She was a very cute girl when all was said and done, and any guy would love being with her. I asked Elizabeth to tell Fang that I was taking a shower and that I would call her later. Poor Elizabeth innocently did what I asked. I just didn't wish to reach Fang. I didn't want to interact with her. I even switched off my mobile phone for more than a week. I hoped that Fang would get the message, and I think she did at that moment.

My flight was just a day away, and I was trying to put everything in its place before I left. I arranged everything in my room—my books, drawings, violin. I made my room tidy so that Uncle could use it, for whatever purpose, in my absence.

Uncle made me the promise that he would support me to finish college but that he would like to see me working. I informed him that I would grant him the latter wish, and I assured him that I would handle the former by working part-time while studying. I have always respected my uncle, and I knew that he was not in a great financial situation, even though he owned a small business with his wife.

The next morning, I walked to the public library to return some of the books I had still with me. I cleared my possession of any books from the library and then, just out of curiosity, I decided to take a quick stroll inside and look for any new titles. Surprisingly, I found myself the only person there at that early hour until I met Sophie, one of the girls I worked with in the origami and handmade festival and a close friend of Fang.

We greeted each other, and she asked me about my visit to the library. I told her about some books that were in my possession. She asked me about my plans after high school, and I told her (just a lie) that I would be stuck in the city and would start some sort of business there. She asked me then, for whatever reason, to search for her for a book by Stephen Covey, *Effective Leadership*. I knew the location of the book, and I think she knew it also, but still I acted dumb and followed her to search for something she had already found. She looked so hot in my eyes! She may not look the same now under the same conditions, nor had she looked at all pretty yesterday or the month before, but she did at that particular moment.

The wild, long-numbed animal started rising inside me as my eyes captured Sophie's small round ass. She was thin enough, but the jeans she had on were even thinner. I just couldn't imagine how she would take them off later or how she had put them on in the first place. The small visible part of her abdomen and back grew bigger as she reached with her hands to get a book a few shelves up. She asked me for help, but I refused, with the excuse that I had a shoulder pain. I enjoyed staring at her bare skin as she kept trying to reach the book. I have no idea why young girls put on such dresses in the early hours of the morning. No average man will molest a woman unless she invites him, and Sophie was making gestures of invitation. From my side, I never had any objection to seeing young girls with such lovely tight dresses; it had always been a pleasant picture in my eyes.

I swallowed and let my desire a little loose. My fingers reached across the narrow space separating us and touched her bare lower back. Sophie paused without saying anything; she just inhaled in a lot of air—a gesture which, combined with her silence, was a pure sign of happy invitation—and I started rubbing my fingers against her skin. She turned to me and pressed her lips against mine. I embraced her thin body, and my hands started roaming all over her clothes, and then underneath. She helped me with this part, and in a minute we were in a heap in a corner, with me on top of her. In less than fifteen minutes, we were over, consumed. She was smiling widely at me, so happy at the pleasure I bestowed upon her.

In a split second I suddenly felt a shadow walking behind me. I turned and could only see part of the dark-haired girl passing by. My heart pounded a little as my lips whispered "Fang". I lifted myself off Sophie and hastened to the end of the rack. Yes, my heart was correct: it was Fang. She walked quickly out of the library, and looking at the bright sun-lightened wooden floor, I could see a few tiny wet drops. I realized Fang was crying. She had a crush on me. I had no intention of walking after her and giving her some explanation that would just be a lie. I didn't feel any obligation towards her to do so. I just let go.

"Who was that?" Sophie asked. She approached me and held my little finger.

"I got to go," I said. I felt disgust for Sophie now. Her open-neck orange T-shirt wasn't fully adjusted, and nor was the bra underneath; one nipple almost popped out of the hanging bra.

"I will be always available for you," she said, to my surprise. "I want to start it properly this time. I am breaking up with my boyfriend now. I just want to be frank with you from the beginning."

Her words seemed somewhat humorous in that situation, but I didn't wish to comment on them. She slid then a piece of paper in my palm. I opened it and found some numbers.

"Call me," she requested, with eyes full of joy and hope.

I smiled and walked out of the library. The animal inside me became numb again after being fed, and I had no feeling whatsoever for Sophie. I could see that she built a lot of bridges based on just a quick, casual episode. As I walked pass a garbage bin, I threw the piece of paper in.

8

$g$iven that my mother was Chinese, I didn't find it difficult to merge in with daily life while studying in China. There were many students in my college from India, Pakistan, and Vietnam. I was glad to see such diversity in the college. In my class and my major, there were four students from Vietnam and two from India. My complexion carried just a shade of my Chinese origin, while the rest of my looks leant towards the west. I found it very easy to talk with students from different cultures.

My major was mostly focused on programming, but I still studied other subjects such as project management, business, mathematics, and English. Though my father was a programmer, I didn't know anything more than usual about it, but I had the will to learn and deepen my knowledge. The programs my father had once developed were kept safe with me, and I continued to check them from time to time. Though I hated to hear anything about my father, I still didn't wish to remove those programs of his.

Though many of the students found the subjects a bit difficult, I embraced them easily. Our courses started with programming algorithms and the basics of computers. Then followed subjects like Visual Basic 6, Java basics, HTML, ASP, ASP.NET, JSP, PHP, Visual Basic.NET, C#, Oracle, and then advanced Java programming. Courses related to hardware and networking occupied a smaller portion of our studies, like A++ and Network+, and those related to general subjects, like English and math, occupied an even smaller portion.

The programming courses were of great interest to me, and I used to do my own extra research about each topic in my leisure time. I never limited myself to what the teachers used to explain. My Java instructor, a young Japanese guy, called me a genius and always held me up as an example to encourage other students do their best. I was informed later that this instructor already had a business in Japan and that teaching was just a source of extra income, something that accommodated his life-long interests and complemented his other activities.

My Visual Basic instructor, Howin, a Chinese lady in her late thirties, used to depend on me to solve issues and errors she would be asked about by the other students, either in my class or another. She would note down the issue or the error and tell her students that she would be bringing the answer later. Whenever she couldn't solve it herself or when she didn't have enough time for it, she would bring it to me. Because of her ignorance, she didn't realize that one learns more when faced with issues to work on solving. I was glad of her dependency on me; in the end, it was benefiting me and increasing my knowledge about the subject. But I must say the instructor was pretty; she took good care of her body and skin and she didn't look like the mother of three kids, but she was.

Most of my instructors were just dumb in my eyes. What else would you say about people clinging to life so strongly and yet not doing their best to justify the salaries they receive? I used to help students in the classes, those having issues in their programming assignments and projects. If there is no instructor available to help, should the students fail and waste the money they spent for the course? The instructors, seeing the fact that there was an internal instructor in the class, took it for granted that I would always help my classmates.

Even though I didn't try to make friends during my studies, many students were attracted to me. I believe it was a gesture of thanking me for giving them a hand when asked. Otherwise, most people don't like to approach someone mysterious like me.

There was one Vietnamese girl who always asked me for help. She always used to sit in the back row in the class and was a serious quiet girl. I never intentionally tried to look directly at her face or figure, nor did I ask her name, but I became aware of her anyway. She was a small-figured girl, and she was always late for class. I got to know that her name was Trinh from the instructors calling her name almost every day when she came in late. She wouldn't call me for anything, but when she saw me getting up from my chair and trying to help other students, she would bug me. Only then did I glimpse her tiny skull, which was always rainbow-coloured with makeup, the sight of which warded off any boy from approaching her. As I was explaining any topic to her, I could sense her eyes all over my head.

My inner self didn't quit talking to me about girls, and what encouraged that was the sight of lovely girls all around—in the college, the college library where I did my part-time job to finance my studies, in the market, on television, and in my day and night dreams. Lovely creatures were everywhere, and many would just approach me here and there. My complexion was something of interest for many girls. Some Chinese teenage girls would pass me and drop their eyes on my well-shaped chest or would circle my muscular arm with their hands. My body had always been in good shape because that I never quit going to the gym. Most girls like to talk, always have something to say about someone. When the Chinese girls talked about me, they referred to me as "Charming"

But no girl bugged me outside the classroom more than Qiuyue. She was a regular customer in the college library. I didn't know her at all. She was really cute, to be honest, and very hot. She always wore a knee-length plain flared skirt, which she had in four colours (alizarin, antique brass, candy pink, and white) and a semi-fitted T-shirt with short, slightly ruffled sleeves, shirred and cooped in front, and with a slight shirr at the centre back. Again, I noticed that she wore only four colours of the same T-shirt: gold, light blue, bubble-gum, and black. It was as if she was sponsored by a particular fashion brand. She would wear the same skirt or T-shirt only after the cycle of four had been repeated. I recall when she first came to borrow a book, she was with a friend of hers, and I could see them whispering to each other while their eyes watched me. That day she borrowed a thick book about economics and just smiled at me. I thought then that she was studying economics. Two days later, she returned the book, but she was alone on this visit, and she took a book related to accounting. Before leaving, she asked my name and where I was from. I gladly answered and gazed with joy at her slim figure as she walked out. She would come in on alternate days, borrowing different sorts of books about politics, literature, surgery, and so on, apparently without realizing that borrowing such a diversity of books at short intervals didn't make any sense. With each visit, she would ask me a question about myself. It was like an interview that lasted over a month. Finally, she bravely stood in front of me one day. I looked at her and reached out to take a book from her hand, when, to my surprise, she put her hand in mine. I lifted my eyes.

"I am asking you out," she said. Her bravery was so weak that that her lips were trembling.

"Okay," I tenderly smiled at her.

Now, she was shocked by my instant response. I could read it clearly in her face. She was wondering what to do next, as (I could tell) she wasn't quite prepared for immediate acceptance from my side. She put her hand in her small purse that was in the shape of a single flower, and took it out in haste and then repeated the action twice before I interrupted.

"Can I have your phone number?"

"Yes . . . yes." Her voice trembled. She started mentioning her number. She would pause for a while in between and excuse herself and then correct some digits over. That day was the only day she would leave without a book in hand. She was so embarrassed.

As I left the library that day, the image of Qiuyue kept coming back to my mind. Inside, I was laughing at her nervous behaviour and the way she approached me. I could tell now that she had intentionally been visiting the library just to get to know me better. I took my phone out of my pocket and dialled Qiuyue's number. Though it was almost eight-thirty in the evening, I didn't feel shy calling her as she was the one who had approached me.

"Hello," came her soft voice, and it seemed to be followed by an unusual question mark.

"This is Gerald."

"Hi . . ." she said in a broken voice, and I could sense her getting nervous all over again. I heard her saying something to someone, which was followed by the sound of her footsteps.

"Hi," she said again.

"Did I call at a bad time?" I questioned, thinking about the delay between her first and second answers.

"No, it's never bad a time for you." She spoke with some rhythm.

"When shall I see you?"

"See me? Oh . . . when you are free? Okay, next . . . next . . . ," she said.

"Next?" I echoed.

"Next week, Gerald. Is it fine with you?"

Of course it was. Why wouldn't it be?

"Yes, and?" I was waiting for full details rather than small scraps of information.

"On Tuesday. Next Tuesday we shall meet. At nine o'clock in the evening near the Starbucks opposite the college."

"Okay, beautiful." I complimented her before closing the line.

I entered my small room and locked the door behind me. The wall was decorated by paintings I spent nights on; they were directly on the wall without any canvas or other material. I painted greens—trees, flowers, and gardens. Some of my books were arranged in one corner of the room, and on the opposite corner was my collection of origami, the centre of which was a grey paper vase with a bouquet of yellow paper-made flowers.

I tried to fill my life with things around me, but could fill nothing of fulfilled joy within myself.

9

$\mathcal{T}$uesday came. Qiuyue had stopped visiting the library, contrary to her normal habit, since the day she had asked me out. By eight, I locked the library. The old librarian, Shun Zun, had great trust in me for a reason I didn't inquire about. I had full authority in the library when he was not around, and he had requested me to take, in his absence, any necessary decision required for the best interests of the library. I remember once I asked a young guy to leave the library as he was harassing a girl who was doing some reading. Later I found out that the guy was the son of a rich family, and when the college director summoned me, Shun Zun stubbornly talked to him, saying that if I was to leave the college, he would do so as well. Old Shun wasn't just a well-respected figure in the college, but also in society.

"You have great management skills," he told me one day, adjusting his round, thin-rimmed, Harry Potter-like glasses with his pinkie finger—the gesture which I remembered more about him than any other and the gesture which brought humour in class, as some students used to imitate him.

Shun Zun resembled a typical old warrior from ancient times. He had thin, steep eyebrows that added on his angry-looking face, in addition to the V-shaped curve in the area in between those eyebrows. Three or four thin hairs dangled just below each side of his cheeks, and those were his moustache. In his thin-lipped mouth, he hung a pipe that looked like it belonged to Sherlock Holmes.

I walked to the gym locker, where I deposited a few of my clothes, and met a few gym-mates, mostly Chinese. They greeted me and asked me whether I was joining them that day. I excused myself, saying that I had a date, which presumably was true.

"Yes, man," Bojing giggled, demonstrating his white teeth. Then he hit me mockingly with the back of his fingers on my abs. "She is a Chinese, isn't she?" He kept giggling.

I smiled and nodded.

"Fuck you, man. Be careful of the hair, ha!" he finally said, taking off his shirt and walking to the swimming pool. His six-pack abs were well shaped, and most of his back areas were muscles.

Bojing was a good guy and very hard-working in the gym. He was the first guy I got to know upon joining the college gym. He used to help me in my weight lifting even though I didn't ask him for any help. I didn't know much about him other than his great sense of humour and his dream of being a model in the future—when he had time for it, as he said. He told me a few times that many teens and ladies of his country were keeping thick pubic hair. That's where his last statement came from. He told me many times that he had experienced swallowing a couple of hairs while eating the cunt of a girl.

I changed my dress and put on some floral cologne. I picked out the bouquet of paper flowers I had made a few days ago, and a book. I locked the locker and walked out.

I reached the Starbucks coffee shop within five minutes. I checked my watch. It was still only twenty past eight; I was early. I decided to stop at the nearest lamppost and read my book while waiting for Qiuyue. Only then did I see the thin statue-like body, standing with her back against the lamppost I was walking towards, and her black hair drawn on the left side of her shoulder, thus revealing the right side of her olive-skinned neck. I was sure that she was Qiuyue even before seeing her face because of her outfit that I had already memorized—the same T-shirt and skirt. This time she was wearing an alizarin skirt and a gold T-shirt, with simple green slippers in her feet. "How bad she is at choosing colours!" I remember thinking at the time.

I walked up and stood directly behind her. Still she was unaware of my presence. I reached my hand and lightly pinched her milk-white naked neck. She started and jumped. I started laughing as she turned and looked at me with grim eyes and with her upper teeth tight on the left part of her lower lip.

"You are early!" she said.

"You are early." I smiled and looked at her face.

There was something different in her. Only now could I see a tiny dried black pimple on the left lower side of her jaw. But that wasn't the thing I found that I liked. It was the glasses she was wearing, black-framed clear glass. It was the first time I had seen her with the glasses, but she looked really different, much sexier than she was already, as it added touches of new beauty to her white complexion.

She saw me now staring at her eyes.

"Oh, I should take them off." She looked down as she put her fingers on the outer edge of her glasses trying to take them off.

"No," I said, and I put my hand on her shoulder.

She stopped, but the glasses were already in her hand now as she looked at me. Her eyebrows lifted up a little in an attempt to understand my meaning.

"They look good on you. You look prettier with them."

She blushed and said nothing, but she sure was happy. Her eyes fell on my hand.

"This is for you," I said, presenting her the bouquet of paper flowers I was carrying.

She took the bouquet from my hand and looked at it all over. Then she laughed.

"Where this came from? I like it!"

"From my garden," I answered quickly.

She looked at me, and again her eyebrows lifted, asking for clarification.

"I made it."

She didn't make any more comment about it but just pressed it lightly close to her chest. Now her eyes moved to look at my other hand. She took the book from my hand and read the title, *Switch Bitch*. She asked me why I was carrying the book. I answered that I hadn't expected to meet her early and thus I had planned to read until she came.

"So where do you wish to go?" I asked, taking the book from her hand.

"Wherever you will take me," came her simple answer.

I paused for a while to think of a suitable place. The idea of taking her to a nearby bar came into my mind, but I discarded the thought as it looked a cheap idea given that Qiuyue was a very shy person. The idea of taking her to a good restaurant wasn't on the table, as she confirmed that she already had her dinner, though I didn't believe it. I remembered seeing a cinema not so far from the college, and it was showing a good movie, *Love in the Time of Cholera*, which was based on the magnificent novel by Gabriel García Marquez.

"Cinema?" I asked.

Qiuyue nodded with a smile.

We rode the first bus, which stopped just a few steps away from the cinema after about seven minutes. We bought tickets and a small box of popcorn and went in. We were just in time; the lights in the hall were turned off and the movie started. Qiuyue started eating popcorn, while I held the box in my hand. I was staring at the big screen, but my focus was half slyly turned to Qiuyue, who instead of watching the movie, was staring at me, thinking that I was in ignorance of her gaze. I made no motion to make her think otherwise. I could see that the girl had some liking for me. I liked her too. When I turned my head to her, she would turn hers too, but to the screen. I kept doing so many times for the sake of forcing her to watch the movie, or at least a little of it.

The movie had some sexual and nude scenes. Whenever a scene of this type would come, I could glimpse Qiuyue turn her head left and right to look at the youngsters, boys and girls, hugging and making some noises. I realized she was wishing for some intimate gestures, and so I put my arm next to hers and lay my head next to her head and then lifted it back up. She looked at me and smiled. She understood my implications and wrapped her left arm into mine.

She started to give more attention to the movie, as it was getting really interesting, until there came one scene where I could sense her embarrassment, as she was confused whether to look at the screen or drop her eyes into her lap. The scene was when Fermina, the main female character, came into the bed of her husband, Juvenal. The husband tried to put his hand on his wife's bosom. Qiuyue decided to look down into her lap, trying to conceal her blushes. I was sure that she wouldn't show the same shy blush if she happened to be watching the scene alone. It was the sweet shyness of sharing sexual thoughts, ideas, and scenes with someone of the other sex, especially a newcomer into one's life.

I liked her character; it seemed so sweet and shy, even if that shyness wasn't completely genuine. I told myself that it was a suitable moment to intrude into her with some gesture suggesting my lust for her. Frankly speaking, although I did like her at that point, physical satisfaction was what I sought most from Qiuyue.

I slyly freed my hand that was wrapped by Qiuyue's, and moved it down and stopped as it touched her flat tummy. Only then did I see how soft was her slightly velvet T-shirt. Then I brushed my hand against that soft wall. Her silence there meant a green signal for me. I glanced at her lap. There was my gift, the flower bouquet, resting in tranquillity. My fingers crawled down, under the bouquet, and just parked there. She gave a small quick shiver but kept silent. I leaned against her side and pushed my hand a little further down, and my fingers touched the end of her skirt. In a few seconds, my palm was on her left thigh, and the cloth of the skirt started folding and getting pulled upward along with the movement of my hand. My fingers tapped and danced there on that soft surface. I looked at her. There was a movement in her throat that came from repeated swallowing, but she didn't look at me, only up and to her right side. The soft dancing of my fingers on her thigh provoked a soft dance in her feelings as well. I knew that she liked to be caressed like that and she didn't mind it; she was just shy. The tips of my fingers were just near the end of the thigh, where also the end line of her panties curved.

The movie ended, and so ended my caressing. I prayed that this had aroused some sexual desires in her. I never was the type to initiate asking any girl to sleep with me. I had my pride about that, however strong my lust for sex.

We came out the cinema, with her walking slowly (slower than when entered). She tried to avoid looking at me, and so her eyes would look down or at the bouquet of flowers in her hand.

47

"How will you go home now?" I asked.

"I . . . will take a taxi. There are plenty here." Then she heaved a nervous sigh. "Can . . . drop me home?" she asked. "I am not used to going home alone late at night."

At first I thought that she would ward me off in her way, but now I could see I might get my way with her for the night.

"Yes, sure," I replied.

We stopped the first taxi, and Qiuyue mentioned the address. Within twenty minutes we were at the gate of the building where she lived, but unfortunately she was already asleep with her head resting on my shoulder. I paid the taxi and woke Qiuyue up. She looked like no more than a child to me. She yawned as she got out the taxi and walked inside the building, pulling me behind her with my hand like a trolley bag. She just waved at the old watchman when he asked her if she was all right, and I was left with the responsibility of explaining.

"She is a little drunk," I lied, and the old man held his hands together under his chin with a big toothless smile.

We walked to the elevator and took it up to the third floor. The corridor was dimly lit and the smell of Chinese food was everywhere. Qiuyue unlocked room 301 and stepped in while still holding my hand. She really looked drunk. I saw that it was just one untidy apartment, but clean. She walked then inside the only bedroom in the apartment and sat on the scrambled bed.

"Will you sleep beside me?" she said simply, to my shock.

I stood in front of her and looked down at her face. Her eyes were struggling to keep fully open. I wondered for a while if I might have given her some drink by mistake or if she had taken any. She was now a totally new character, compared to the one I had first got to know. She had suddenly broken all her barriers of shyness and dragged me inside her apartment, and now she was asking me to sleep beside her! I couldn't understand what was going on in her head. I was scared that she was under some unpleasant spell.

"What about your family?" I asked. "Do you live alone?"

"My mother is not home tonight. I am living with Mom only. Don't worry about that."

Then, just ignoring all my comments, she lay down in her bed on her right side. There was a small space still unoccupied at her back for me to fill. But before anything else, I walked back and locked the apartment door, which she had left half open. I took off my pants and T-shirt and tidily hung them on the back of the door of the room. I slowly put my hand on the bed, which produced a small crack, and then I lay beside that strange creature, as she seemed to me. But nothing of her weird character mattered. I just missed the touch of a girl's skin and sweet body aroma.

I pushed my body closer to her and put my hand on her arm and then through her sleeve to place it on her shoulder. I sniffed through her hair with my nose touching the scalp. My hands caressed every part of her sensitive body, and with each touch she shivered as if a slight electric current went through her. I took her clothes off, one piece at a time, starting from top to bottom. A small naked butterfly was in my arms now, a child disguised in the form of a mature girl. I embraced her tightly against my body and kissed all over her face. She welcomed each and every action with ecstasy, but blocked it in front of me when I tried to charge her from the front and finish the task there. I was filled now with a certain embarrassment that she had been in my arms for more than ten minutes and then prevented me from getting my manhood's utmost end pleasure. I started withdrawing my body from her, but she held it and stopped it there. She turned to her right side again, leaving me against her smooth bare back where the upper bones stood out vividly. Her left hand moved down to her buttocks, where she indicated for me the back door. And there it ended, with our desires ending through that door. She perspired heavily and was damp in her our wetness, but it all ended peacefully.

I held her with a tight embrace. It is so amazing to hold a beauty in your hands, and my beauty then was more or less like a child. For one instant I found myself liking her and wanting her, that strange small creature of nature. I put my lips on the back of her neck and sniffed there and closed my eyes.

I found myself like a boat floating freely and aimlessly on the shadow of an open sea. The memory of my father's murder came into my mind in front of my eyes. I just refused to open my eyes. I kept them tight shut looking at my father standing in front of me, smiling with a piece of human heart in his hand. My body started getting tighter and tighter, and with force my hands started pressing against Qiuyue's body. She struggled and, from fear of hurting her, I withdrew my body.

My heart was pounding. I got out of the bed and covered Qiuyue with a blanket that lay improperly folded on the floor. I sat naked on the floor next to the bed, with my back against the small black drawer on which were scattered a few of her school books.

I shed a few tear drops. Peace and tranquillity crawled again into my being and dropped a dark curtain in front of my sight.

10

$\mathcal{F}$ootsteps were moving around lightly. I could sense it and feel it though my eyes were closed. I let my eyes open slightly, and now, with my head bent and my chin touching the hollow of my chest bone, I could see female feet just a few steps in front of me. It took me just a second to recollect where I was. Breezes from the ceiling fan were hitting against my bare thighs and the back of my neck.

I thought for a while that it was Qiuyue, but lifting my eyes along the tight slim legs, which seemed a little bigger than those of Qiuyue, my eyes reached the chest, where two humps proudly stood and alongside the head, little curled hairs dangled on each side of the small hills of the chest. Only then, without even reaching the cheeks, I could see that it was someone else. Yes, it was a little older and heavier version of my night-mate, Qiuyue.

I gazed at the face, almost motionless.

"I am her mother," came a whisper, carrying the same tone of voice as that of little Qiuyue.

I was totally naked. The image would have been absurd, weird, even rage-inducing in some other situation, but it was so simple with that woman standing in front of me, with her eyeballs rolling inside their narrow space and flashing at me, every visible inch of me.

I didn't feel any embarrassment at all, but I realized it might not be so appropriate to be seen in such a position in front of a mother, any mother. I didn't know what time it was then, and I was waiting for this newcomer to move out so that I could move freely. But she didn't.

"I don't know how it can be that you sit there and sleep while a girl is awaiting you in bed," she commented. Her gaze now dropped to my muscular chest. Her expression could not hide the definite lust that was painted in her eyes. "Go on, give her a hug." She was referring to her daughter. "Come on." She waved her hand, requesting me to rise to my feet.

She wasn't blind. She could see me sitting naked there, and yet she firmly stood in front of me and made such a shameless request. I could see what she wanted. I granted her the scene she longed for—that of a nude muscular male. I didn't feel even a bit of shame with so shameless a lady. I could see with my conscious mind, her eyes pricking me as I calmly stood and moved under the blanket and next to Qiuyue.

The door closed then, and before that the one light in the room was turned off. My eyes remained open for several minutes. The damp but sweet, fragrance of Qiuyue's skin was allotted for my zest; my nose enjoyed sniffing it again and again. It is beautifully cosy lying next to a handsome girl.

11

$\mathcal{T}$he small bouquet of feelings I had developed for my childish Qiuyue started to evaporate over the next few weeks with the heat of my melancholy a bit a time. As days passed, I could see nothing in my heart for her but an absolute pure lust.

But I kept in strong touch with Qiuyue. She poured some dim light of happiness into me that my soul lacked. Our night-time affair was reduced to its minimum, especially when we both had exams in the way. Still we would go to the cinema from time to time. (No more caressing was needed from my side to awake her gentle numb animal.)

What bothered me about the new development was her mother, Ah Cy. She would call me from time to time, sometimes even in the middle of the night, asking when I was expected to visit her daughter and her again. To be honest, the daughter didn't call me as many times as did the mother. I couldn't understand what she was expecting from my side. Did she expect me to hug her and kiss her with her daughter there near her, I wondered at the time.

I always answered her calls and answered her politely, but she bugged me in my personal time. I saw that she always tried to start conversations with me, but I always put an end to them by saying that I had to go and that I was busy. (She knew it to be a lie, but who cares what she thought?) I was embarrassed to tell Qiuyue about her mother's calls and intentions towards me. However bad I am, I never tried to break people's family bonds.

It was a Sunday night when my cell phone rang to indicate I had received a new message. I was sitting in front of my laptop with three windows of Java code open; I was working on developing a Snakes game for my Sony Ericsson cell phone. I was in the last stages of developing the game, which I spent more than two months on. (The first had been spent studying the Micro Edition of the Java programming language, something that wasn't taught to us in the college, where only the Standard Edition of Java was taught, and that lightly.)

Like father like son. Yes, you may say so, but for me it was just a passion to learn something. Sometimes I would just wish to be far better than my father in the field he might have mastered the most.

Before going to bed that night, I picked my cell phone. (I normally did so to set morning alarm.) There I saw the new text message. It was from Ah Cy. Seeing her name as the sender irritated me, but what filled me with surprise was the content:

"Those whom the Gods love grow young. Happy birthday."

At the end of the message she posted a smiley face. How did she know about it, I wondered. I didn't get a call from her daughter for the same purpose, and I didn't get any greetings from anybody else. How the hell had this lady found out about a day I happened to just forget?

I didn't mind it. I ignored it. It was the whim of a woman with some emptiness in her life. Otherwise, who would bother to remember days from other people's lives when their own lives demanded more attention? I didn't reply to the message, not even with thanks.

The next day when I reached the college, I headed to the cafeteria. I used to have my breakfast there two or three times a week. I took a cup of coffee and one egg sandwich with no mayonnaise and no cheese. Whatever little oil the sandwich contained was more than enough for the consumption of my body. I just hated to spoil my body's looks for trivial reasons such as filling the small silo with a load that later would get discarded in the toilet. The days when I didn't go to the cafeteria, I would have my breakfast at home—two egg whites for the sake of the four grams of protein they contain, and a glass of milk.

I went to the cashier, but the usual lady, who was in her fifties and who knew me, wasn't there. In her place was now sitting a younger version of her with brighter colour and a much smaller shape. I could only say she was tastier than my breakfast. I wouldn't really have minded having her for breakfast instead if offered the opportunity. She looked me in the eyes while I tried to avoid gazing at her. I took out my wallet and paid for my breakfast and then, with a smile, tried to walk away.

"What is the major of your studies, sir, if it is all right for me to ask?" came her polite voice, forcing me to pause there near the counter desk.

I gazed at her for a while, and her face was all cosy smiles. I gathered myself and opened my mouth in an attempt to reply, when all of a sudden Trinh, my Vietnamese classmate, appeared from nowhere just near the counter, her eyes holding fire that was strongly turned on the counter girl. My eyes turned from the natural fine-coloured face of the cashier girl to the synthetic, rainbow-painted appearance of Trinh. Trinh slapped, as it seemed to me only, her tray on the counter desk. I could see the cashier girl stir for a while and put one hand on her chest. I just walked away and took the nearest table.

I held the cup on my tray. It was so hot that the heat bit my pinkie finger, which was always the nearest to the hot liquid in glass containers. I spread my pinkie finger in a ninety-degree angle and circled the top rim of the cup with four fingers. I took the first portion of a sip. I always liked the aroma of milk.

As I put the cup back on the tray, the chair opposite to mine was pulled out, and there was Trinh again. She put her red tray just parallel to my brown one. I glimpsed at our trays; they were perfectly in line with one another. Trinh sat down rather noisily as she pulled her chair back in under the table. I looked at her face, and she gazed back directly into my eyes. I turned my eyes away and had a small bite of my sandwich. When I raised them again, I was met with the same gaze. What was different in the scene was her small-lipped mouth that was chewing on some pieces of fruit. Her small eyelids blinked more frequently than normal, but beautifully, winging over her dark eyeballs.

"Such girls, eh," she said after almost two minutes of silent gazing. "So poor and naïve they are." Her eyes were directed at the new cashier girl, who was handling another customer now. "The first day they get a job; the second they search for a catch."

I could follow her meaning, but I didn't know what business it was of hers. I caught a glimpse of her tiny jaw bone. A small dark spot was stained on the upper part of the right side of her neck; it looked like the remains of an old contact with flame. Her earlobes carried long dangling earrings, on the ends of which were gathered small greenish-grey ovals that generated a nice rhythm when put in contact with each other.

While she was staring at the cashier girl, I kept examining her face. I think she was the only girl I knew in the class without a partner. She was always alone. I never saw her even with other girls for a long period of time. She walked alone, sat alone, and dined alone. The thought had come into my mind that she might be a lesbian, otherwise what sane girl in a diverse open community would paint her face like that and keep every guy away from her! She was a source of laughter for my classmates and a source of jokes for the instructors, but she simply took it all with a calm soul. Once our programming teacher, Howin, was discussing during a break period about aliens and a program she had watched the day before on the National Geographic channel about the subject, and in the middle of the discussion she referred to Trinh as an alien. The whole class (whoever was there in the break) laughed, including Trinh herself, but I didn't. It is so hurtful to mock one another in their presence.

But honestly, didn't Trinh know that girls are the objects of passion and art? Didn't she realize that feminine influence has a stronger grip of power on us men than that of devils?

Her long eyelashes flapped. I couldn't determine whether they were original or false, but I inclined to think the latter. The tops of her eyelids were painted in thick violet. The cheekbones were flushed in pinkish red and the small lips were thickly painted in shiny brown. How much time did she allocate for painting such a portrait, I wondered. And there was her hair, dark ash blonde, with so many braids, some interchanging with each other, but delicately designed. I remembered seeing a small girl in a mall some time ago with the same hair style.

"Why you are so upset with her?" I asked and then lowered my eyes to my cup of milk.

She kept silent for a while, but again her eyes were fixed on me.

"I am not," she answered.

We went back to our silence and both tried to finish our breakfast. I realized that she was a fast eater. After finishing, I noticed her open her small bag that was strapped on her right shoulder and lay on her left hip side, and, to my surprise, she took out a long piece of chalk. She broke it in half, returning one half to the bag while the other ended up in her mouth!

"See you in the class," I said as I gathered myself and walked away from that strange girl.

I entered the class, but for the first time ever it was empty, although only five minutes remained until the start of the class. I occupied my seat, lifted the lid of the desk, took out a notebook, and started sketching. I recalled the message of Ah Cy about my birthday. The message served as a reminder that I had been in China for almost two years. That meant I was twenty, which meant that I was spared to live for eight more years. Another thing appeared in my mind: my house, which once used to be my father's house. During those two years, I had not even seen my old home, for which, all of a sudden, my heart was homesick.

Students started coming into the class room and flashing me smiles as they passed me. I just ignored it. Then came in Howin, followed by Trinh. The former was holding a round tray of cake, and the latter two small delicately wrapped boxes.

"Happy birthday!" Howin gave me a big smile as she put the cake on her big square desk. Some of the students gathered then, putting together four student desks and then helping the instructor to shift the cake.

"Happy birthday, Gerald," came random voices from my classmates, some soft, others thick.

I was sitting on my chair, motionless. I could see what was going on, but couldn't see why. I turned my eyes to Trinh. She smiled at me, and the ends of her lips stretched wide. I noticed now a nice small line on top of her cheekbone, and the only reason I discovered it at that moment was that Trinh was a person who rarely smiled. Suddenly, I received a small wink from her.

My gaze was only on Trinh. I saw her as a different person now, more beautiful than the clown face she put on. I think she noticed me gazing at her. She turned her eyes to the left and right to make sure that she was the only object in the range of my gaze. She blushed; I just could see it through her white-powdered face.

Howin approached me now with the two small boxes, which just a minute before I had seen in Trinh's hands. She put the boxes on top of my desk.

For half an hour my classmates and Howin celebrated for me. I didn't care much about the celebration, and one class was already wasted for it. They brought in soft drinks and potato chips and shared them between themselves in the classroom. Trinh was now nowhere in front of me. I turned my head and saw her sitting quietly on her seat, having a small piece of brown cake; her gaze was floating on me.

I didn't like it either to move out my seat and celebrate madly with others; I just sat still. On the desk I arranged the two wrapped boxes. The wrapper papers were so shiny and colourful and decorated with childish objects. They were so displeasing to my eyes. I slowly pushed them aside on the table, putting one on top of the other, fully aligned. One of my classmates approached me with a glass of coke, and I asked him about who was behind arranging the celebration. He told me that it was Howin; she had collected money from the students, bought the gifts (of which only Howin knew the content) and the cake, and arranged for everything to be a surprise.

Howin was standing behind her desk, her mouth chewing in slow motion, and her narrow eyes fully concentrated on me. Despite her age, she was a hot beauty.

Thinking about it, what had forced this instructor to put even the slightest of effort into arranging that party for me? I could understand my classmates contributing money for the celebration, the reason for which would be that I helped them when needed in their assignments. But what could explain Howin's initiative?

How girls love to remember things we, men, see as trivial!

12

_I_ was twenty years old. Oh, how time moves so fast! It seemed only yesterday that I left the United States, and now two years were over—two years out of the limited lifetime that lay in front of me, two years out of the journey that seemed long for me, but was surely very short for most people.

I stopped contacting my uncle and his wife, but being better persons, they continued to send me many letters asking about myself and the status of my studies. During those two years, I sent them only two replies to say that I was doing fine. Don't misunderstand me, reader. I carried no sort of hard feelings for the most wonderful couple I have ever met. They were my sky and earth. It was only that I had this feeling that I needed to ward off anything related to my past, and my uncle and Elizabeth represented a big portion of it. Everything related to my past brought me agony and echoed in my emptiness with loud screams to get rid of this life I held within me. Memories of my heartless father and unmotherly mother were already thorns in my heart and aches in my mind.

I couldn't discard those ashes of memories that kept blindfolding me from embracing, joyfully, the present glimpses of happiness that were floating around me.

People around me were like objects I had to use to survive. I didn't need them, but they added colours to the black and white portrait of my life. It is like oxygen that you inhale; it is important to you only because you need it to live. I admit that loneliness is a deadly weapon and its effect is faster than many lethal poisons. I did adore my solitude even though it was really killing me slowly, but living among humans did reduce its deadly effect. That is not to say that people amused me to an extreme extent; that never happened. Long interactions with people bored me to death, and crawling to my solitude was tantalizing that boredom with arrays of thoughts, mostly dark ones, about death and God.

Though Uncle Eugene was a very religious person who did not drink, I wasn't. I don't believe in God and could never see any real purpose for adopting a belief that you grew up seeing people around you adopting. My uncle and his wife used to go to church every Sunday morning and would stay long praying to God. I would be dragged with them, but the only reason I put up with attending church with them was to show my respect for them, not for their God. They were faithful Christians, and I do deeply wish from my heart that they will meet the destiny their hearts long for. For me, God is a fantasy ship in a stormy sea with the promise of salvation, but he does not exist in my realm. It is just a portrait of a ghost, an angel with so much beautiful colour only when looked at from afar. When you approach it, it is nothing more than some trick of the eye. If God is there, then why do we suffer? Why do we end up suffocating in a life that we loathe to behold? Why doesn't heaven give us another chance to choose a new, gleeful, and useful course for ourselves?

Sometimes, I just think of the path my life might have taken if there had been a happy alternative to my family experience. What if my mother had been a good mother? What if my father hadn't killed her? What if they had chosen each other based on true love, which I know nothing about?

I just try to work up my imagination an attractive scenario for my parents. My father chooses the path of his brother and tries to marry at an early age in the full belief of love for a girl he used to physically see, meet, and know. This girl might be a family member or she might be a stranger, but she is one whose social welfare is well known to the society and to the people around her. Elizabeth, my uncle's wife, approaches my father, along with my uncle, and tells him about this girl whose genteel character speaks about her in society. My father refuses the well intentioned initiative at the beginning, but as days pass, he finally agrees under one condition: that he will see that girl first in person without her realizing who he is. My uncle and his wife agrees to that, and Elizabeth, knowing the girl briefly already, calls up on her and invites her for dinner with her husband; there is no mention there of my father. As the girl accepts the invitation, Elizabeth invites my father as well. Then comes the dinner night. Father, Uncle, and Elizabeth are seated on a pre-booked table, while a chair is empty awaiting the promising girl.

My father hasn't given her enough attention and her promising personality isn't well established in his mind, but everything changes at the moment of the meeting when the girl approaches the table, dressed up in full red, her delicate long fingers wrapped around a red purse, and her long light-brown hair gathered and poured on top of her left breast. Elizabeth goes now against her plan and doesn't introduce one to another, as their eyes are already commuting some secret message of infatuation. This brief meeting leads to a gentle affair between my father and his new girlfriend. This affair smoothly flows to the bond of engagement, which finally engulfs them under the kiss of marriage. The couple share their deepest secrets, and they both show gratitude for each day spent together. The fruit of the holy relationship is me. I grow under the lovely warm wings of parents that every child would heartily demand. I fall in love with life and get around me bunches of loyal friends who love me and whom I love. I love being alive, and every day of my life is bliss.

This is the image I wanted for my life and my childhood. Why didn't I have it? Is it not a noble request to ask for this humble favour? Am I so greedy asking it, or should I be even more polite asking it? Why doesn't heaven give me this privilege of picking the course of my life, when the god of gods will hold hands with me, supporting my demand?

Who is to blame for the foggy shadows of dismay that cover my life? Is it Father for being so naïve and making the wrong decisions in choosing a wife and then killing her? Is it my mother for being unfaithful in her heart and seeking her own benefits? Is it me for being the son of my parents? Or is it God for putting us all together in the centre of a volcano, knowing that it will explode at the end and spare none?

13

"*W*hen is your birthday, Gerald?" Qiuyue asked.

She was sitting opposite me in KFC having dinner. It was her decision to go to that fat-filled junk food restaurant. She said that she missed it.

I turned my eyes to her in surprise, hearing the question. Her eyes were fixed on her tray. There was on one side a small mud of mayonnaise mixed with tomato ketchup and on the other end of the tray lay a bunch of French fries, the look of which disgusted me with the sparkling fats covering them. While I had a vegetable burger, she had only the fries, and she said that it was her favourite. I just wondered how she kept her body so fit after all swallowing all that big chunk of fat!

But the question she asked seemed dumb to me and a little surprising. It was surprising because last week, on my birthday, I had got a message from her mother greeting me on the occasion. How come the daughter missed it while the mother didn't? I had believed that the mother got the date from her daughter, but now it seemed my theory was wrong. Qiuyue was sitting with one leg atop the other, with the leg on top bare-footed as the green slipper lay on the floor. Her legs seemed shiny. I could see now that apart from her physical attraction, I loathed her.

I think almost two weeks had passed since last we had intercourse, and I had my lust in my throat now. I slipped my hand under the table and started caressing her raised foot, moving my hand up her leg slowly. She looked at me with that childish smile on her face, covered her lips with two fingers, and giggled. After a few seconds she shook her leg and pushed her chair back a little to escape from my hand.

"You are burning me hot," I whispered and she giggled again. "Away, away . . . not today, Gerald, I cannot." Then she leaned towards me on her chair and whispered, with both her hands on her lap, "My vagina is paining me today."

This may have seemed a good reason to speak of, but looking at the facts, she had never allowed me to have her from the front, and now she was speaking of her genitals that I had never consumed. I don't know if she did figure out her wrongly given excuse. Whatever reason it was, she didn't wish to sleep with me that night.

I accompanied her to the bus stop and waited there with her. As the bus arrived, she kissed me and got in, but before the bus took off, I called her.

"You missed my birthday this year. We will celebrate it together next year," I told her.

"Okay," was what she managed to say.

I walked to my apartment alone. It was a quiet night out, and I liked it. The air brought a chill into my bones.

The first thing I did when I got home was to remove my T-shirt. There was a little pain in the bottom of my chest. I opened the door of my closet and stood in front of the square mirror attached at the back of its door. I pressed the left end of my chest and felt the pain. That day was the first time that I had carried eighty kilograms for the chest exercise. Bojing, my Chinese gym-mate, gave me good support for my exercises, and I helped him in return. He was a talkative guy, but he would talk within limits, unlike some who, when they talk a lot, talk more lies. I could see he was a good guy at heart. He would always talk about sexual relationships, but again, he would talk within boundaries, and I was always surprised at his deep knowledge about sexual issues. He seemed very bright to me in spite of the foolish image of himself he portrayed in front of me. Whenever I asked him whether he had a girlfriend, he would answer that he hadn't. I didn't believe him in that matter and believed that he wished to keep it concealed from me, for whatever reason. He was handsome, to be honest, and I could see him achieving his dream of being a model, as he had once told me.

Suddenly there came a knock on my door. I think it was the first time, since renting the room, I had heard anyone knock on my door in the evening. I looked at my wrist watch; it was nine thirty-five. It might be someone who had mistaken the address, was the thought that came to mind. I opened the door and there stood in front of me the last person I wished to see at the time, Ah Cy.

She was wearing a sleeveless mini-dress that was beautifully shaded in lime green and aqua blue; the former colour starting from the top, and the latter from the bottom, and the colours gradually radiating to lighter shades as they grew from the both ends of the dress. Above her waist, just below the breasts, there was wrapped around her a light-blue ribbon. So elegant, she was! So neat, she looked! I could see she was better than her daughter at choosing colour combinations. Her slim legs were twinkling; I guessed she wasn't sweating; she just oiled them or rather creamed them up. Her calves looked strong and suggested the owner to be a lady who plays sports. She stood at my door with one hand on the door frame and the other straightening her already straight hair. Her mild perfume was so weak and yet charming.

"Are you busy?" she asked with a tone that would raise hundreds of suspicious questions.

I hesitated to answer at first. Her eyes were scanning my bare chest. Two of my neighbours were passing in the corridor now and they started whistling with their eyebrows uplifted. The bright aroma of Ah Cy's perfume was a little clouded by the bad smell those two brought with them, and I guessed it came from their mouths. One of them winked at me, and the other made the shape of a circle with one hand's thumb and index finger, and started pushing his other index finger into the circle.

"No," I answered Ah Cy to avoid the strange looks from damned people such as those two passers-by.

But before I even asked her, she stepped in, brushing her arm against my chest. I closed the door behind her. She stood and looked admiringly at my painting on the wall. She asked me about it and whether I drew it. Then she looked in my open laptop, and she made an unfunny joke about the written lines—whether they were some sort of an ancient lost language or some sort of secret code.

"It is a MIDlet application I have been working on for about a month."

"Okay," she replied, not understanding what I was talking about. Her eyes were rolling all over my small room.

She stopped near the bed, stared at it for a while, and then sat down there in a relaxed mood with her hands stretched backwards. Instantly my eyes caught a glimpse of her white panties through her legs that were uncrossed in the style of a man.

"Did my daughter sleep here ever?" she asked, her fingers pinching the mattress.

"Once," I answered honestly.

Suddenly she moved her arms and rested her elbows on her knees. Her hands crawled under her dangling hair that was now covering her face and her forehead. I couldn't understand what she was up to and what she sought, but I could hear her now inhale deeply through her wet nose. She was crying. I stood there in front of her. I didn't know what to do really, but I didn't plan to do anything. I wasn't a babysitter or a comforter to offer refuge to anyone having personal issues. I believe that every person has some issues in their lives.

Ah Cy raised her head up a little, but it still was curtained by her silky hair, and she wiped her under eyes with the bottom of her palms.

"Sorry for that," she said with cracked voice. "I am supposed to have a date tonight, but the guy is busy with another girl, much younger."

She pushed then her hair back with her hands and started smoothing it. Her wet eyes didn't look good to my taste, and I tried to avoid them. It was only then, as I lowered my eyes that I caught a glimpse of her nipples. What a daring lady she was to put on such a nice outfit with no bra underneath!

"I am sorry for that," I said. I had nothing to do with her personal matters.

In a split second, she jumped from her place and wrapped me with her hands. What a surprise! Her wet cheekbone tickled the side of my neck. Her short nails pierced my back, and her breasts were flattened against my chest with the force she put into that embrace. One hand then moved down my back and rested on my buttock and pressed there. I stood motionless with my hands parallel to my sides.

"Give me this night," she said in what sounded like a whisper.

I was hungry for sex at the time; I had always been hungry for soft creatures. As I mentioned earlier, I hadn't had intercourse with her daughter for more than a week. This period might seem very short for some, but for me it was long enough to revive my need for sex in its strongest form.

"Can you?" she whispered again, but it seemed more like pleading this time.

I said nothing but answered with a series of actions. I placed one hand on the centre of her bottom and pressed it hard down there. My other hand cupped her breast and squeezed it gently like a sponge ball. She liked that, I could see it, and she drew back her chest a little as I pushed my mouth there. She pushed me onto the bed, and I let myself fall to satisfy her. She sat on the floor and like a snake she crawled near me, spreading my legs apart as she did so. She disarmed me of my pants and underwear, sliding them under the bed where I hid some of my shoes and unwashed socks. She started kissing there in between my thighs and licking and even chewing, as I felt it. My genitals were under her full control, and she liked to be the dominating one. I don't know how long she sat there doing some ritual I guess she had mastered over years of experience; I couldn't feel myself, and how could I, being with a lady with such an experienced mouth? My soul was drawing away from my body, and all my nerves fell tense. I sensed the veins on my neck harden. I don't know if I screamed there or not, but I can say I moaned. After that first batch of extreme caressing, she stood on her feet and pulled down her short dress, which fell at her feet, and followed that by pulling down her panties. She stood naked now. She came atop me, and her magic fingers worked again to apply the required touches. I felt myself so smoothly sliding into her with my wet genital, like when one slides a wet candy into his mouth. Thinking of it, the smoothness of the candy's sliding motion can be explained by the amount of saliva in one's mouth and the amount of wetness on the candy, and it can also be explained by the width of one's open mouth. In my case, I believe the second example applied more strongly with Ah Cy. She did what she liked with my body, and I was, happily, against my own will giving her my whole physical self.

About forty-five minutes later, we lay next to each other on my small bed, our soaked arms touching.

"Please don't look at me as a bad mother," she said.

A moment of silence hung in the air. I didn't comment on what she said.

"I love my daughter, and I hope that what just happened will be kept as a secret between me and you," she continued.

I laughed inside myself at her talk. What a good mother she really was! So lustful and sexually greedy to want a portion of what her daughter had found. What sort of a family life did that woman lead, I wondered, and what a shining example she had set for her poor daughter! I still didn't say anything but just kept silent, looking at the ceiling where the white fan, edged with thick dust, moved slowly as if out of energy.

"My daughter is not fully sane, eh? Those are some harsh words," she started again. "Don't you know anything more about her? I suppose you don't, and Qiuyue will not reveal it to you. I suppose she just cannot." She paused for a couple of seconds. My eyes were still turned away from her, and no single word did I speak. "She lost her father when she was just eight. My boyfriend was such a good guy, and if anything wrong happened in his life, then I suppose it was me. We had such good intimacy with each other. He was ready to marry me, but I wasn't, even after getting pregnant with Qiuyue. I really loved him, and, to be honest, no man ever came into my life after him for whom I felt stronger love than the love I felt for him. I was just scared of getting married. It is such a big step in life. I believed it requires much preparation and planning, and I had done none of those at the time. My boyfriend accepted my decision to delay the marriage plan till the day I was ready. Qiuyue grew up more with her father than me. You see, he was a better parent than I was. He was responsible and caring, with a lot of love to give out. Qiuyue was strongly attached to her father, something I didn't mind because I was always busy with my girlfriends. Going out with them and having chats and beers was my normal life. But the day came when my daughter and I were to lose something dear. I was called one night to hospital and found my daughter in a terrible state; she was emotionally broken. She had been walking out with her father that night, when a speeding car hit him so hard that he instantly died in front of her eyes. My poor daughter could never recover from that shock, but she sought for something as atonement for that loss. She sought for an alternative love in males. It was a desperate search on her side. I could see that she would have been tricked very easily by boys disguising their sexual lust with fake words of love. To avoid any unexpected results from her desperate search of love, I advised her privately not to give her vagina to any boy unless she was sure of his true love for her."

Ah Cy paused here and sat on the bed, and pushed herself to rest her back against the wooden palate at the head of the bed.

"Qiuyue agreed to that because she believed in what I said, but still I wasn't fully comfortable with it. Then I got this idea: to let my daughter fall in love with a guy I chose for her, and what's better than a guy who has no interest in girls, a gay?"

I frowned now upon hearing that and turned my eyes to her. I caught sight of her beautiful bare breasts, uplifted without even the support of any bra.

"I contacted one of my girlfriends who used to know a few gay males from her neighbourhood. She arranged one for me, and I insisted on meeting him first. The guy looked good, and he has a strong muscular body like you. His name was Bojing, and what a funny character he was! He even told me that he was planning to be a model one day."

Bojing! Yes, my ears caught the name and everything she described about that guy fitted the Bojing I knew from my college and gym, except what she mentioned about him being gay.

Ah Cy went on. "Qiuyue soon fell in love with Bojing as I planned for her. Bojing was a very good speaker, and he did his magic with my daughter, but he hadn't the slightest interest in her. I paid him well for his role, but in the end I had to put an end to Bojing's role in the life of my daughter; I was running out of money to pay him, and his continued existence on the stage for long would ruin everything. I made him tell her that he had to go to the United States to finish his studies and that he would return to her as soon as he was done. And thus it went. Bojing was out of sight, and Qiuyue was dreaming of the day she would meet him again and get married to him. That was four years ago, and you, Gerald, are the only person in her life with whom she had casual sex since the supposed departure of Bojing. I am sure my daughter didn't give you her vagina, did she? Eh, she will not, I am sure of it. My daughter always finds emptiness in her life, and then you come to fill it up."

"But why would you put this illusion of love in her mind?" I asked.

"I don't know," she said and lowered her head. "I suppose it is a mother's quest to protect her child. However bad a person I am, I am a mother in the end, and I carry love for my child."

A cloud of sadness came over her expressions. She got off the bed, grabbed her dress, and put it on, before combing her hair with her hands.

"Thanks for having me in tonight." She smiled now and left my room.

What a strange mother she was, but I believe she was a better woman than my mother. But saying this, I didn't consider Ah Cy a good mother and woman. I could see that she brought destructive ruin to the lives of her boyfriend and her daughter.

What a strange family I had met. Having the privilege of sleeping with both the daughter and the mother! Who would believe that? What could one say about having access to the mother through the front lids and the daughter through the back cave! I couldn't see what principle of loyalty they both believed in.

What bothered me more than the mother and daughter was hearing about that paid-for Bojing. Was he the guy I knew? A gay!

14

Since the day I heard the story of Qiuyue, I started avoiding her and she, for whatever reason, stopped bothering me. I was glad for that. For matters related to my sexual fulfilment, the mother, Ah Cy, was there. I could see how careless a mother she was. She didn't deserve the good things in life. I was enough for her to fulfil her unfilled desires—me, a bad guy and half her age. Looking at her, I just wondered what types of girls exist in life and how far they will go to satisfy their needs. It was really a shame that Ah Cy was a mother. She would visit me afterwards on a regular basis in my room, fulfil her need, and go. I didn't bother asking her about her daughter; I believed the mother targeted just one particular pleasure by visiting me, and I sought the same from her.

A few more months remained for me to finish my studies at the college. Shun Zun, the old librarian, started getting sick and grew worse every passing day. I was under pressure to stay longer hours in the library on a daily basis. That meant having less time to study for my exams and less time to spend on my MIDlet application that I had been working on for more than a month. I intended to enter the competition that would be held in the following month. I couldn't refuse to stay longer hours in the library; it was my main source of income, as publishing poems and short stories didn't bring me much to feed myself with. Thus, I started bringing my laptop with me to the library to work on my MIDlet application. I realized that winning in the competition would be lucrative for me for the financial benefits I would get out of it.

Having such a timetable kept me away from the gym for a while. This meant that my curiosity to learn the truth about Bojing and his story with Qiuyue remained unsatisfied.

While Qiuyue stopped approaching me, Trinh did not. Whenever I had breakfast in the college in the mornings, she would sit with me and eat hers in silence with her gaze full on me. Sometimes she would bring her breakfast with her and sometimes she would even bring some for me as well. I had tried beef noodle *pho* and pork-mixed *banh cuon* with her.

"How is your girlfriend?" she asked me on one occasion.

"Who?" I wondered.

"That . . . that Chinese girl?"

"Qiuyue?"

"I don't know," she said.

"She is just a friend of mine. She is not my girlfriend," I answered honestly.

Trinh smiled when she heard my answer. I could read in it some sort of triumph. It was true that I didn't feel anything passionate about Qiuyue anymore.

The day for the MIDlet competition came and I was ready for it. My application was fully functional and was applicable for most types of Nokia and Sony Ericsson mobile phones. The application was a car-racing game that could be played by a single user or a maximum of three using the Bluetooth utility for connection in between them. My programming teacher, Howin, was the first person to see my application before registering it in the competition, and she greatly liked it and admired my effort. After registering my game in the competition, she announced the news in the class, saying that I had made a great achievement by entering a prestigious competition and that success in it would bring pride to the college as no other student had done it before.

A few days later, the results came out. My application won second place in a competition in which participation had come from colleges and universities throughout the Far East. This brought some sort of happiness to me, but not as much as gaining some money for my own future. But it did bring a reason for Howin and my classmates to start a new celebration for me. Trinh gave me a gift of a nicely stitched handkerchief, and Howin gave me a kiss on my cheek in front of my classmates. I did wish that all the hot teachers would give us kisses as rewards for our excellence instead of throwing out some meaningless words of appreciation.

My daily talks with Trinh, mostly at breakfast time, tickled in me a slight feeling for her that I couldn't analyse. Her rainbow-coloured image started to reflect differently now in the mirror of my eyes. Her image slowly unveiled a disguised beauty that I believed that she, for some reason, veiled intentionally in the first place.

It was a Monday afternoon when I finished my class and walked fast to attend the library. Realizing that I had left the book I was reading in my bag, which I had dropped in the early morning in the closet of the gym, I walked quickly out through the open yard where the sunlight was fading. I unlocked my closet in the gym, took out my book, and locked it back up. Walking out of the gym, I paused at the end of the corridor near the glass windows that opened to the swimming pool. I saw the most unexpected form of a girl I knew. Trinh was getting out of the swimming pool wearing a dark blue swimsuit. Taking a towel, she started rubbing and drying her hair. She looked so different and very unlike the Trinh I and everybody knew. Her face was wiped up clean, and her true beauty was unveiled now with the layers of makeup peeled off.

My gaze couldn't keep away from that pure copy of the messed-up image I was used to seeing. As she approached the glass door and put her hand on the handlebar, our eyes met and she panicked all of a sudden, but she stood her ground, unsure of what action to take. It was as if a deep secret was revealed in a moment of mistake. I grabbed the handlebar from my side and pulled the door open and smiled at her. She put the towel back on her head and walked quickly into the ladies' section.

The next day Trinh approached me as I was having my breakfast. She was gasping, and the full array of disturbing makeup was back on the nice young face I had seen yesterday in its natural beauty.

"You shouldn't tell anybody. Did you tell anybody?" She was staring at me, still gasping.

"What?" I smiled, examining her face for a spot that might have missed the thick white face paint.

"What you saw yesterday." She swallowed now.

I started brushing the top of the table with the tips of my fingers.

"I saw nothing of you yesterday," I said with a smile. "Yesterday, I saw a beautiful young girl in her full blossom."

Trinh blushed and lowered her eyes, dropping a shy smile there before walking away.

*   *   *

Only one month was left until the end of my college year, and still I hadn't satisfied the burning pleas of my soul to visit, just once, my old home, my father's home once. I didn't know what had become of it, but I secretly wished to know.

Slowly, Trinh and I started to get closer to each other. All of a sudden, I felt that I had found what my heart longed for, something like the same feelings I first sensed with Qiuyue. I was glad to have been the person privileged to see that lovely face of hers in its true form, and she didn't wish to reveal it to anyone else. From having breakfast together, we started sharing our lunches. And then, she stopped annoying me in class and ceased asking me silly questions to get my attention. She wished to pull me closer to her, I believe, and she had got it now. I was so close to her that I had the right to hold her hand and walk with her and even kiss her on her cheeks at the end of the day. But she hadn't changed her style and dress, and nor did I ask her to do so. I just enjoyed being with her. My classmates, even Howin, gradually stopped making jokes about Trinh and her appearance just out of respect for me.

Then came the news of the death of Shun Zun. I was asked by the library manager to work full time in the library. I still remember the belly of the guy, the manager; it was rounder than that of a pregnant woman in her ninth month. He was pushing me to take full responsibility for the library. How much of a fool was he? I explained to his deafness that I had got exams and then the end of the year. I wouldn't get stuck in between those narrow racks of books, despite the love I had always carried for books, like that old man. That fat man couldn't see that my flaw-full life was being swept away a bit each day. When I firmly rejected his offer, he sent me off and from that moment my part-time work ended in that library.

Having no other job to do any more at the end of my classes gave me more time for myself and my studies. I spent more time with Trinh studying together. One afternoon I invited her to come to my room to study. She hesitated for a long while, and I liked her honest hesitation, but shyly she agreed in the end. I respected her more for that.

That day, we studied for two hours. Then I suggested her that I should draw her picture. She giggled with pleasure and instantly stood on her small bare feet. Then, raising her heels and stretching her hands up in the air with her chin lifted up, she formed the pose of a ballerina dancer, and she really did look like a ballerina dancer with her thin delicate body. There we abandoned our studies, and I, with my skilled hands, took my drawing pad and sketched out her overall figure. From where I sat, I could see traces of tiny hairs on the surface of her silver hands.

Afterwards, we were sitting together joking and laughing when there was a knock on the door. I looked at my wrist watch; it was now almost eight forty-five. How fast time had passed, and how much we had enjoyed ourselves together! This girl, who looked like a freak in the eyes of others, was so amazing and such a fine-natured creature of heaven.

I walked and opened the door to see, to my unpleasant surprise, Ah Cy standing there wearing a slim white dress, a little slimmer than her body, that displayed clearly the shape of her bra and the lines of the black panties at both sides of her hips. She lifted one side of her lips in what seemed to be a half smile, and small lines of age stretched under her eyes. I didn't smile back. On that evening, only then, my lust didn't bubble up upon catching sight of her sexy body and complexion, even though she was as nicely put together as ever that night. Everything in me was just shallow, plain, so grounded to the ground. I could sense Trinh peeking to see the visitor, and Ah Cy at last glimpsed her and thus started to pull back her almost fully developed smile.

"I think I should leave you now," Ah Cy said, but the end of the line seemed more like a question mark than a full stop.

I didn't reply, and the visitor pulled back. That was the first time I had sent her off without fulfilling the purpose of her visit. When I closed the door and turned my face back to her, Trinh turned her face as well, but away from me pretending to be busy. I sat next to her on the floor while she silently wondered slyly about the visitor, but I, understanding the situation, was not generous in providing any details.

"She looks beautiful." She simply commented, playing with her maroon coloured nails.

"Is she?" I replied. "I don't think she's any prettier than you."

Her mouth opened a little, but no word came out. She didn't smile at the compliment. I knew she must have been thinking that such words were what I usually said to any new girl I met. Again, I was miserly in providing any explanation. But there our conversation about Ah Cy ended, and so did my relationship with her.

As it was starting to get late at night, Trinh began collecting her books and materials and stuffing them in her bag.

"I'd better go now. It is ten already," she noted.

"But you can stay here tonight. It is already late." I suggested without looking at her.

She paused and hesitated for a couple of minutes, thinking and analysing the situation, before whispering her agreement. She asked for a glass of water, and while she drank it, she slyly put a piece of white chalk in her mouth. I didn't know whether it was out of hunger or habit, but she assured me in words that she wasn't hungry. In the bathroom, she squeezed the toothpaste onto her left pointer finger and started brushing her teeth. But when she came out, the full range of makeup was still covering her face. A small drop of water lay on her dark pink-shaded cheekbone. I reached my finger, but she drew back her head, but still my finger reached her face and wiped that wet spot. She smiled as I removed my finger and realized what I had done, but my eyes were focused on that spot that now was set clear and showed the original colour of her skin. It was like wiping a dusty window to see the beautiful face of nature beyond.

I lay on my narrow bed, facing the adjacent wall. Trinh came and lay next to me in a very slow motion. I didn't feel having the courage to turn to her and caress her in any way whatsoever. She looked very pure to me, and that filled me for a while with shame of even thinking of removing that innocence from her.

"You are not scared of my face?" she asked in a light whisper.

I was glad she had witnessed her own ugliness with that hand-made clown face of her.

"I am not scared of disguised angels," I replied.

I heard her silent giggle through the noise of releasing air through the nose.

I closed my eyes and, I don't know after how long, I could hear some echo of Trinh asking me to come with her to Vietnam. I couldn't figure out till later whether it was just a dream or a real request.

15

*W*ith my small bare feet, I walked on the dark green, fresh wet grass. My pants were folded down, and so the grass played around my ankles. I walked fast in a way similar to running. My small dark-grey bicycle with training wheels lay aside. I just glimpsed it and passed by it. The door of the home was half open and my mother's hands were stretched out, waving for me to come and give her a hug. On the doorstep, there was a light-brown teddy bear with a pink ribbon around its neck. With a wide smile on my face, I murmured words that couldn't be understood even to me. But then the hands started withdrawing inside the home, dragging with them the teddy bear. As I took further small paces now, I could hear strange noises, something like a groan, soft and hard. The smile was still on my face, and the promise of the happiness that I would be finding in the laps of my parents far exceeded the glimpse of fear those groans planted in me. My soft bare feet touched the surface of the cold tiles on the doorstep. I walked in, and now warmth started creeping into my feet. I turned my eyes to my feet, and the softness of the muddy stuff under my feet and its red colour filled me with joy. I leaned down and fixed both my open palms next to each other and then dug them inside the warm material and came up with a handful of it. With the thick liquid dripping slowly from my hands, I walked forward and with my head pushed the slightly open door of my room. I could hear my father's voice murmuring some prayers. Then Father's voice was calling for me. I came in, and what struck me first was the colour of my room. It had changed to match the dark colour of the material in my hand. Suddenly I felt my body getting wetter and wetter with sweat. I was frightened by the sight of a human organ on the floor near the big brown-booted feet of my father, which were not spared the stains of the colour of red. My body was sweating more and more, and fear was creeping up to my heart. My father was smiling and reaching out his hand for me. His hand was covered in the same material that I cupped in my hands. I shook my head, refusing to obey him. My body was heavily sweating and shaking. I closed my eyes tight.

I opened my eyes and shivered at catching a glimpse of a clown face on top of me. It took me a couple of seconds to recognize the face of Trinh. My heart beats started slowing down and getting calmer as I heard the voice of Trinh telling me that I was having a bad dream. I wondered at first what she was talking about, but feeling the dampness of my clothes brought back the memory of the nightmare. I sat on the bed and shook my head. Trinh sat next to me, stroking my hair and touching my wet scalp and telling me over and over that everything was fine.

"What time is it now?" I asked.

"It is six," she whispered, as if afraid to wake me up fully.

"I am planning to visit my home," I said, laying one hand back and resting it on the bed.

"Can I come with you?" she asked, as if knowing what I was talking about. She was already in my room and I couldn't understand what she made of my suggestion.

"Do you want to?" I asked.

"Yes," she simply answered, and the clown feature on her face forced a smile on mine.

I leaned and pushed my body out the bed, placing my feet on the floor. There I was surprised by a sudden kiss on my jaw. I could sense the paint on Trinh's lips touching my skin. I gave no sign of any pleasing reaction though the kiss was a comforting one, especially after that nightmare I had had. Feeling embarrassed, Trinh moved away. She sat near her books, arranging and rearranging them. I could see that she had woken up much earlier; her face was well made up. For a couple of seconds I sat contemplating her face from the side view. She sat there like an angel with no visible wings, and I felt the desire to embrace her tight to my chest, with all the innocence of the world, the whole of her innocence.

I washed up and had a quick shower. I came out the bathroom with only a towel wrapped around my waist. She glanced at me and I noticed it, but as she turned her face away, I turned away mine also. I started putting on my clothes, and I could sense her eyes on me, slyly concealed behind the act of going through my drawing book.

"Who is this?" she asked.

I was putting on my green T-shirt when I heard that question. Pulling my T-shirt down my waist, I turned my head to see her smiling at the sketch of a woman standing with her head turned, waving with her hand as if waving for a photographer when realizing that her picture was being taken.

"She looks beautiful," Trinh commented.

I had sketched that picture a year earlier. Yes, the lady in the picture was waving to a photographer. The lady in the picture was my mother. The sketch was based on a real picture taken by my father in my early childhood. I remembered it, even though vaguely, despite my young age. We were on a beach that sunny day. I was sitting on the yellow sand playing with my small toy cars when I heard my mother's voice calling my name as she was walking towards me. Turning my eyes, the big smile on her face caught me. At that moment, my father's voice came calling for my mother, and she, with a gentle toss of head, gave him a sweet smile and got the flash from his hand-held camera on her face. Actually, the picture was framed in my room in my childhood house, and that was the reason I had it fresh in my mind.

I walked to Trinh and put my hand on the cover of the drawing pad, applying a slight weight to close it. She looked at me.

"She is a dead demon. Shall we go now?" I said.

She pushed the drawing book into my hands with the tips of her fingers and nodded her head.

Outside, the light sun rays gently pricked my eyes. I blinked fast a few times, and my eyeballs became watery all of a sudden. Like a silent clown, Trinh giggled and made some comment about me being like a prisoner who sees the sun for the first time in ages. I seemed a little worried, but the presence of that girl beside me soothed things in my heart.

She started to sing in a whisper what seemed like some comforting rhythm. I didn't pay any attention to it; my mind was busy building expectations of what I was going to see and feel once I found my old home—if it was ever meant to be, standing as it was in its old spot.

I reached my hand and wrapped Trinh's fingers in mine. Her fingers shivered at the first touch, but when they calmed down, her whispery song calmed and stopped. I stopped a taxi and when asked about the destination, I requested the driver to just follow my directions. Trinh looked through the window most of the journey, while I was busy looking at the streets, some of which remained the same, unchanged; even the pale painted shops along them still stood, bearing some scars of age now.

There was the toy shop, my favourite one in my childhood. Once my eyes glimpsed it, it was hard to turn away from it. The glass window was still so clear that I, although in the cab, could clearly see inside. I glimpsed the shadow of the old sales lady who used to always give me candy whenever I visited it with my parents, saying that I was the most exquisite child in China. A new generation of small toy characters was on display behind the glass window. I had given up on them already and considered them now very trivial. It was hard for me to recall all the names of my own collection of toy characters.

There was the tall building where my father used to work—on the fourth floor that was allocated to the private

IT company he worked for. The building had survived the ravages of time and had been given a slight renovation: the white paint had been replaced with stripes of pink and yellow, and the small windows had been given square frames. I remembered when my father brought me to his office for the first time. His colleagues joked with me a lot, while I was nervously shaking inside, mainly out of fear of their scary complexions. Some of them jokingly asked my father to reserve me for their daughters. One of them even asked me whether I had a girlfriend.

On the corner of a different street was a small bakery shop, whose name was engraved on its wood-board, *MEMORIES*. At this point, Trinh turned her face to me and smiled, pointing with her finger to the shop and whispering its name to me. She noticed what I noticed. Yes, memories were revived there of me walking with my mother, she holding my tiny hand. We used to visit that bakery twice a week, and my heart longed to sniff in the fresh smell of the warm bread it produced, but that feeling I suppressed.

The last station on the memory chain was the graveyard, *LIFE* (as it was titled), which, my uncle mentioned, contained the graves of my parents. It looked so lifeless and gloomy now with its bushy trees, some of which were just skeletons of trees.

I asked the driver to stop at a corner; I had reached my destination. My eyes were looking at the place now, the area where I had grown up and spent the early days of my life. I put my hand in my tight pocket and took out some cash. I didn't remember when I had put those notes in my pocket, but I did find some, and I don't know how many I took out, but I am sure the amount was more than what was asked for by the driver, because when Trinh and I left the car, the driver called me and mentioned something that his voice didn't carry enough force to drop into my ears. I was in a different state of mind now.

The area in view looked desperate for change now. It lacked life and looked like it had no spirit left to keep it standing. No damage had been done by any human deed, but nature had its dirty hands over everything. The green grasses that once filled the area were so brown and black now that one would hardly believe they had ever been alive. The trees had no leaves, and their bodies were filled with ugly cracks. Even the pavement carried deep lines of age, and some parts were totally broken. All the homes I used to know in the area still stood there, but they were more like ghost houses. The barking of dogs was loud enough to disturb the lifeless silence.

"Where is your home?" Trinh asked.

I turned my eyes and gazed at my home.

"There," I replied, pointing only with my eyes.

Trinh didn't make any comment. She just followed me as I walked. I stood in front of the door and put my hand on the handle. The door was locked. My hand was covered with dirty dust that released some black taint. In my mind came the picture of my mother putting a key under the square flower pot on the patio. I asked Trinh to wait there, and I walked to the patio I recalled. The key was still there. How surprising it was! I returned and unlocked the door.

I felt a big onslaught of memories rush over me. I closed my eyes quickly as the image of my father walked in front of me, passing me and walking to his room. Another image came of my mother sitting on the chair watching television. I felt somebody place a hand on my back.

"Are you all right?" Trinh's voice came.

I opened my eyes and nodded, but my legs were a bit heavy. On my left were three rectangular windows, the one in the middle taller than those on each side. The once pure and plain white panel curtains at the top now looked light grey. I caught the end of the curtain panel of the middle window and pulled it out with force, and there I heard Trinh's gasp of fear. I soothed her with a gentle smile as I dropped the curtain on the floor. I did the same with the other two curtains. Pure rays of light were now slipping inside in front of my eyes with sparkles of dust floating in them, drawing bright squares in the overall dark landscape.

"It looks better now," Trinh giggled in whisper.

She dragged each of her flat boyish shoes on the floor like a child, leaving clearly traceable marks in the layer of husks and dust. That generated a disturbing noise, but I wasn't in any state to comment on it.

I walked to my room and pushed the door open with my fingers. The wallpaper still struck me with its beauty as it had done in my childhood. In the damp sadness of the whole home, my room alone seemed still bright with its dim white background upon which scattered rectangles of light colours (pink, yellow, and blue) were printed, and each rectangle was framed in thick unbalanced straight lines of light brown, and the scattered shapes bore sketched flowers in the same colour as the frame. My bed, shaped like a red car, was still parked in the same spot as in the old days, and the funny face on its front still bore a wide smile. I located my toy characters' storage cupboard. I opened one door, and particles of dust were blown from its top onto the front of my hair and a little onto the top of my nose. I picked out one toy, that of Princess Snow White, and turned to see Trinh standing in front of a picture on the wall next to the door. That picture was of my mother, the same picture on which my sketch had been based that Trinh found in my drawing pad that day.

"Let's leave," I told Trinh, and I placed my hand on her arm.

She didn't speak but just smiled and nodded in agreement. We walked out of the house, but a desire still seemed unfulfilled inside of me—that of to visit the kitchen in that now-haunted house, the kitchen that was the scene of a hideous crime that had ignited in me some sort of delicious hatred for life.

I stopped about ten feet from the home and so did Trinh. I put in her hand the Princess Snow White toy and asked her to wait for me at the end of the area, near the first stoplight, which was one kilometre away. The landscape surrounding my home looked a little scary, but its serenity amazed me. It seemed dead inside out.

If anything did echo in my vast inner wilderness, it was merely the dim sensation of some force driving me along.

I paused for a while to see Trinh walking away and then walked back to my home and stepped into the kitchen. The smell caught me—that of dry blood. There was blood still on the floor, and the marble surface of the table was almost fully covered with it except the small area that had been wiped. My mother's corpse lay there once, and reviving its memory brought a hot glow to my heart. I found myself having difficulty breathing now, and my nose was uncontrollably vibrating. Nobody had even made the effort to clean up the mess of my parents. I believe nobody cared to. Looking at the corner where I recalled shrinking into myself when the police arrived caused my heart to miss a beat, and now my entire self was shaking and my eyes were flooding and my nostrils were on the verge of dripping.

I felt a sudden explosion in my stomach and a squeezing feeling of sickness emerged. I rested my back against the corner and slowly let my body slip down there. Now I was sitting in the same spot where I had sat years ago to witness the crime of my father. Scenes came ever livelier now in front of my eyes. Fear grasped my heart, and I broke finally into tears.

Several minutes passed, I believe. I raised my head, and my inner self seemed quieter now, but my anger was enraged. I just hated the home; I hated its presence. I walked around all the drawers in the kitchen till I found a green-handled kitchen lighter. I started walking through all the rooms of the house one by one, throwing flames of fire here and there and ensuring that enough was ignited everywhere.

I walked quickly out of the house and started walking fast straight to where I had asked Trinh to wait for me. The smell of burning garments hung for a while in my nose.

Abdulla Kazim

"Your nose looks red," Trinh said upon seeing me. "Your eyes as well."

She was sitting on the pavement, leaned forward with her legs stretched full in front of her. My eyes fell on the group of tiny red ants gathered at the end of the wide opening of her jeans. I put my foot there on top of those gang-like intruders, and stirred it in a very slight movement that was sure to wipe out most of those gathered there.

Trinh's soft voice crept into my ears, and only now I did give it some attention. She was singing, a beautiful song in a tantalized tone.

Hello darkness, my old friend
I've come to talk with you again
Because a vision softly creeping
Left its seeds while I was sleeping
And the vision that was planted in my brain
Still remains . . . [1]

We took a taxi. I looked back as the taxi started moving. My eyes caught sight of light smoke rising up from the area of my home. My heart bid a hot farewell to my home. I wouldn't visit it again ever, even if the smoke was just fake.

---

[1] "The Sound of Silence" by Paul Simon, 1964.

16

$\mathcal{I}$ had made up my mind to go with Trinh to Vietnam after graduation. My programming teacher, Howin, approached me a week before the end of the semester. I was at the time walking to the gym. She asked me to see her in her office. I walked after her. She had on a very long tight thin-fabric skirt. I could see the cuteness of her small buttocks that fitted her flat body and chest. Till that moment, I had seen Howin as a good person, despite my confusion about some of the signals sent by her mysterious smiles and winks and her casual kiss on my birthday. The perception my mind had created about her up till then was based on the way I saw her with a single eye, but that perception changed when I opened both my eyes on her.

Howin entered the office and turned towards me, reaching her hands back and resting her palms on top of the desk behind her and placing that cute bottom of hers on the edge of the desk. I stood in front of her waiting for what she might say, but in my mind the shape of her buttocks was already engraved. I thought of the silliness of what she might say, and this encouraged my mind to develop the whim of imagining how her bottom might look now, half resting on the desk, and whether, unclothed, it might be soft or (unlike her face) already aged. The progress of my native whim went on, but I guess my face and eyes were on her, just physically, waiting for her to say something useful.

"I want you to stay here." She started, and with this the strings of my whim broke.

Now my attention was with her. I frowned and wondered internally and in silence about the subject of her speech.

"I already talked to the management about you, Gerald, and explained to them how good you are in all the programming subjects. They agreed to hire you as a faculty member. You will help our students make good improvements."

Her speech was so alien to me. I didn't recall having asked her to arrange a place for me in the college. I didn't even remember telling her or showing her any interest in teaching.

"But I am not planning to work in this college," I answered.

I was waiting now for her reply, but, strangely, I saw a half-smile on her face, and the tip of her tongue was playing on the middle of her lower lip. Her eyes were all on me. She withdrew her left hand from her back and placed it on her left thigh. My eyes moved along with that hand. Then that strange teacher came up with an action that totally destroyed any innocent image I had about her and assured me that whatever I had heard from other students about her various affairs with other faculty members was all true.

Howin started pulling her skirt up slowly with her thin fingers, and my eyes caught every lifting motion of that curtain and the revelation of the milky-white marble underneath. My senses all stopped at the next step of that silent deed of her, but she paused now with the skirt up just below her hips. I gazed at the thin part of her white panties that was now visible.

"Come near," she said in a capturing whisper that one can only expect from a woman in bed.

I did what she asked of me and took two small paces towards her. My hot, charged breath touched her face, and our feet gently collided. In a fast motion, I moved my fingers and laid them where they were most desired and expected. Then with a gentle pushing force on my side and a bigger absorbing force from her end, a nasty small smile appeared on her lips, and a little gasp came out of them.

"Yes, I accept your suggestion to work here," I said, rolling my eyes on her small eyes, small nose, and half-wet lips. "But not now. When I come back. I am going to Vietnam." Then my eyes dropped to her bosom.

"With Trinh." Her tantalized tone was mixed with sarcasm. "You love her?"

"I didn't love any girl . . ." I replied, stating it with complete honesty, but then suspecting what I had said in a strange fashion, as the image of Fang Zhang, my first girl, flashed into my mind.

I unplugged my wet fingers from Howin, and she slowly pulled her skirt back down her thighs. There was silence between us now, with a slight smile on both our faces. I turned and went out of the office, closing the door behind me.

I found the story of faithfulness very deceitful. If either of Ah Cy and Howin really believed in being faithful, they wouldn't be enslaved by their blind lust. How strange it is to see middle-aged women chasing young males. What magic youth holds!

I went to the gym, and as I was changing my cloth in the shower area, Bojing came in. I hadn't seen him for a long time and all of sudden Qiuyue's story popped into my mind again, and I asked myself whether he was the person Ah Cy had talked about. The unsatisfied question needed an answer.

Bojing, with his usual big smile, greeted everyone, throwing a joke here and there. He made some dirty comment about a female Chinese movie star and forced laughter out of them.

"I had a very intriguing date yesterday." He started talking about himself. "I met a very young girl in a supermarket, a sales girl, but what a pleasingly plump girl!" He removed his T-shirt and pulled on a sports shirt. "Almost seventeen, Hmmm."

"A virgin?" one guy asked.

"There are no virgins in China," Bojing replied in a joking tone, and everyone in the room laughed again. "But I can guarantee now that she is not anymore."

He then went on to describe her body and some of the bed action they had shared. I walked past him and tapped his back.

"See you in." I said, meaning in the workout area.

"Sure, my Chinese-American friend," he said loudly.

In a couple of minutes, Bojing joined me in the gym. I was doing decline barbell bench presses with twenty kilograms on each side of the bar. It was my first exercise after the warm up. The sensation generated earlier in me by Howin was still having its weakening impact upon me. Normally that weight would seem quite light to me, but at that time it felt a little heavier. After fourteen repetitions, I saw a shadow over my face, and two white hands were lightly placed under the bar, one on each side. I could see the big veins deepen in them at the ends of his wrists.

"Push, push, brother," he said in a voice that I found very usual among people helping each other in gym. It had always been funny for me to hear such tones. It is as if the person, who puts some slight effort in the small help he provides, bears all the burden of the iron weight.

"Since you are here, I say add ten more." I placed the bar in its hook.

Bojing added ten kilograms to each side of the bar and told me to start lifting. I adjusted my body on the bench, and my internal count started with each lift. Bojing's encouraging voice was loud.

"Have you ever had a relationship with Qiuyue?" I asked in a low breath. Then I realized that the question was like a blow. So I adjusted it. "Did you meet a girl with the name of Qiuyue?"

"Let me think . . . I think I encountered three with that same name among my nasty adventures." The volume of his voice went sharply down as he let out the word "nasty". Then he laughed.

"Qiuyue and her mother Ah Cy. I heard a story about an arranged relationship between you and Qiuyue."

Bojing's supporting hands under the bar were removed all of sudden and the full weight fell upon me. My hands felt so weak, but I managed with a big effort to hang the bar on its hook. I adjusted my body to a sitting position and saw Bojing walking out of the workout area. I followed him, and my mind confirmed now that it was he that Ah Cy had talked about.

I entered the shower area. He was standing in front of his locker with his back turned to me. He removed his T-shirt and threw it with force inside the locker and then sat on the bench opposite to it. He rested his elbows on his thighs and clapped his hands in front of his knees. Then he turned to face me.

"What do you want to know?" he asked. It was the first time I had seen him look serious. It was like a mask on a joker's face.

"I didn't wish to bother you," I said. "I am sorry if my question did bother you. It is just curiosity. I just wanted to clarify something I heard before I leave China."

"You heard something, eh? From Ah Cy, I guess."

I nodded.

"That motherfucker mother. Selling her daughter's happiness for the sake of her own. Who would give money to a guy to play with her daughter! I needed money, you see. I know her crazy daughter is very hurt and desperate now, but I am not the one responsible. I felt the true feelings of Qiuyue, and I was sad about it. I wouldn't hurt anybody, but I was in need of money. The mother, unsatisfied with whatever lies she brought upon her daughter, tried even to throw herself on me one night before recalling that I am . . ."

"Gay?" I added, almost in a broken voice filled with shyness.

"Gay," he replied. He lowered his head for a couple of seconds before raising it up again. "But I am not embarrassed about what I am. I am proud of myself. I am sure God is proud of what I am as well. He is the creator." He paused again while his eyes rested on me. I could see thin layers of water in them. "I have tried to change and be what I am not. I wished to be a man with the usual feelings and desires, but I just failed. God hurt me in a very hideous way."

His lower left eyelid was almost full of water. Realizing that, he put one finger underneath it, pressed it in, and wiped it dry.

"A few years ago I thought my desires towards men were just not real and that once I was with a girl in bed, my wild desires would awaken. Based on this optimism, I approached a girl, though nothing inside me was pushing me towards her. A few conversations led us to exchange our numbers. Eventually it all resulted in deciding to exchange our real sexual desires. We agreed on it together and arranged our venue. My inner self told me that I was making a mistake, but I refused to listen. I kept telling myself that I would please that girl, arouse her and give her the best satisfaction, and please myself. I have been watching porn since I was twelve, and I memorized the styles and positions. But once we were alone, the girl did all sorts of seduction tricks she had mastered, but she failed to arouse me the slightest bit. My optimistic venture ended there with her. But I didn't give up there, and I tried a few more times, filling myself with the false belief of being a man. But, you see, nothing worked. When Qiuyue came into my life, I had already given up on trying anymore; I acted purely for money. God left me to the wild." He sniffed, and traces of water in his nose were clear; he was emotional.

"God left me too to the wild," I said and returned to the workout area.

17

*T*rinh was very excited to go back to her country. She said that it had been almost four years since she had left. But I could read nervousness in her eyes as she talked to me about her longing to go back to Vietnam. One day before our travel, she asked me to accompany her to the market to buy some clothes.

It was five in the afternoon when we met at a local post office as agreed. Her style hadn't changed yet, but the white paint on her face was a bit lighter. She stopped first at a shop selling accessories. She bought a few hair ties, hair clips, and head bands. They were just simple black and dark brown. Next she stopped me at shop selling dresses. We went in together. She asked the salesman for some long casual straight dresses. The guy started picking clothes and showing them to her. My eyes roamed around the shop, and one dress caught my attention. It was short-sleeved and floral-printed. I caught it in my fingers and could sense blends of cotton in it. I let my imagination picture how beautifully it fitted Trinh with her slender body, unpainted face, and semi-curled hair.

"Gerald," Trinh called.

I turned my head and saw her coming towards me, holding a dress in her hand. She was about to show it to me when she saw me holding that floral dress.

"Wow, where did you find this," she said, while handing the dress she was holding to the salesman.

She stood next to me and removed the dress from its hanger and held it with her hands from each side of the shoulders. Then she attached the dress to her body and the small hump on her chest bumped out against it. It fitted her as perfectly as I had imagined. She walked to the nearest mirror and smiled to herself.

"Does it look good?" she turned to me and asked.

I nodded. "Aren't you going to try it on?" I said.

She thought for a while, looking at the dress in her hand. I could read the answer from her face. She wouldn't try it on for the reason that it might not look good with her clown-painted face. She smiled at me one more time, but it was a shaky smile.

"I will try it later. I am sure it will fit me. I am content with it."

She bought four of the same dress, but in different colours. She dragged me then to a ladies' underwear shop. I stood outside while she went in. I was a little shy to go in for no clear reason. Trinh looked at me and beckoned me to come in. I warded off my shyness and obeyed her order.

I was inside and just behind her, and yet she kept looking at me from time to time, I believe to make sure I hadn't run away. Going to the bra section first, she stopped in front of a long desk with multiple squares on the top.

Each square section contained coloured collections of a type of bra. There was the trainer bra, the minimiser, the soft cup, the demi cup, the peephole, the nursing, the padded, and the push up. What a big collection! Some of the types I didn't even know about. Looking at her breast size, I would suggest a simple trainer bra without pad, but after going through many of the types, even the nursing one, she decided at last to go for a simple padded one. It was a wise decision, as it would give her small breasts a fuller shape without additional lift. She added to the four bra sets four pink panties—two thongs and two hipsters.

She was now finished with her shopping, and she asked me to drop her home so that she could sleep and wake up for tomorrow's travel. We walked out among the crowd in the market area. With a sudden flip of my head to the left, my eyes caught a shadow of Fang, dressed in dark clothes, walking among the crowd not so far from me. I could recognize her from her side view, plainly beautiful. I stopped where I stood and kept staring at her till she disappeared. My heart beat with some sort of brightness that I wasn't used to, but that brightness faded fast with the belief that it was just a false image of a dead passion.

"Anything wrong?" asked Trinh.

I turned to her and shook my head in silence. She smiled, and we walked together to her apartment. All the way there, my mind didn't stop telling and swearing that that shadow was the real shadow of Fang. I tried telling myself that I didn't care if that person was really Fang. She was part of a past that I had tried to escape, but it bothered me that it proved me wrong. I had to force myself to veil the memory of her in my mind; I was to focus on Trinh and my journey with her.

I entered the apartment after her. A few girls were talking and sharing a bottle of wine. Papers and books were scattered around them. The living room was occupied by those nasty creatures, and they gave us with silent suspicious looks that roused fear in Trinh and disregard in me for their characters. I returned a casual gaze, and the talk among them just fell dead. Trinh held me by my fingers and pulled me to her room.

It was very tidy, her room. The personality she portrayed to the outside world bore no relation to her room. Different sorts of rectangular portraits were hanging on the wall, and they all belonged, I suspected, to the tradition of her country. A small Buddha statue sat on a tiny rack in one corner at the height of my shoulders. Its dark-brown complexion concealed it well in the dark, but its face was illuminated all of a sudden with greyish-green. I could see that it served more than one purpose—as a light and as a religious symbol.

"Don't you bother about those girls," she said, pulling out her bag that was already packed for the journey.

"I am not, but you are," I said.

"I don't want to pick any fight with them."

She unzipped the bag and slid in the new items she had bought without removing them from their plastic bags.

"We will meet tomorrow, I guess," she said, zipping the bag.

"Why don't you come and stay in my room for the night?" I suggested. "It will be faster leaving together to the airport."

It was a very bad excuse, I guess. But I believed that I didn't have to explain it; she would have accepted my suggestion anyway. I needed the warmth of her body for the night, and I got it.

18

$\mathcal{T}$he travel time in the plane was for Trinh just a chance to sleep. She had a brown neck rest placed around her neck in the shape of a funny pig. On the left side, it showed "LOVE PIGGY" stitched in pink. The funny thing about it wasn't the round shape of its ears, but its curly tail that resembled a snail.

Trinh didn't wear any makeup that day, and all the small complicated plaits on her head were removed and her hair fell, semi-curled onto her shoulders. I admit having some unknown feelings for her. She was a rare beauty concealed from others but not from me. No one, knowing her earlier appearance, would ever believe that she was the same Trinh they used to get sick of seeing. She was the pride of my journey to Vietnam.

The night before our travel, she handed me a piece of newspaper just before we went to bed. It contained news about a house set on fire by a stranger. The report was headlined "DEATH HOUSE ON FIRE". It briefly explained the background of the house with a brief of each of my parents and the tragic event that led to the house being abandoned. I could see Trinh having her suspicions about me being part of that torn-up family and being the one accused of setting the house on fire. Her doubts turned into belief as I ripped that piece of paper into very small pieces and piled them under the bed. She didn't ask any more questions, and I didn't provide any free answers.

My one year and seven months stay in Vietnam was a joyful time, during which I worked on a farm and did some paintings of local views and traditions of the country. I also learned there the basics of working with clay, and I started making some shapes, but nothing was perfect, and I was given no chance to perfect them because the old lady I worked with, the owner of a clay-making hut, died, leaving behind that small business to be fought over among her three sons and two daughters; the old lady had always complained about these people and described them as lazy and greedy.

Trinh owned a beautiful little hut among many that resembled it either in shape or design. I used to get confused which hut was Trinh's, and it was only the neighbours' understanding and respect for me that allowed me to avoid conflict, as many times I entered a hut to discover that it wasn't hers. One time I entered a hut and came across a couple who were at the level of intimacy that leads to intercourse.

The times I stayed in the rural area, I slept with Trinh. We shared the same wooden bed with no intimacy. As I said before, I wouldn't approach any girl with my sexual desires in any way unless I was invited to. She liked our relationship to be casual, and I didn't violate her wish.

Her neighbours would ask her about me, and she would say that I was her boyfriend.

The openness of the green landscape opened up the creativity of my paintings. I soon found a shop in the city that agreed to display my paintings, and I was getting paid fair enough for them. Going back and forth to the city wasn't a fast journey, and so, when I was in city, I used to rent a room for stay for a day or more. Being away from Trinh also let loose my attraction towards other town girls, and there were many pretty ones. As always, I was getting looked at with eyes in which I could read attraction.

I never was in peace with the eyes of the daughter of the old man I used to sell my paintings to. Whenever I visited the store, and upon hearing my voice through the thin wood layer that separated the store from the rest of the three rooms at the back of it, she would step in beside her father, and all her fantasies would emerge. On the first few occasions I observed those scanning eyes of hers, I just ignored them, but when they continued to recur, I didn't resist them. It started with me accepting at last the invitation I received from the old man on every visit for breakfast prepared by his daughter. I went with the daughter to the room that served as a kitchen with an attached bathroom. She served breakfast on the table, and then she put her left hand under the cloth on her right shoulder and started scratching a spot there, and slowly the cloth fell lower and lower.

My few weeks of sexual fasting broke there. I jumped to my feet and slid my hand under her long grey-black stripped dress and lifted her up, while my other hand wrapped around her to guide her body from falling but towards me. My lips went searching wildly along the open space of her chest, trying to dive deeper with the assistance of my chin that went clearing the path. Then she spoke, with her hands on my head, but I couldn't get what she was saying. I lifted my eyes to see her pointing at the other room and I understood that she wanted to finish the business we had started in there.

In that position, I took some steps to the room and dropped her body, with a little flip, in the one empty corner my eyes caught. She stood facing back there while I removed all the unwanted layers of clothes. When I went in her, she put one hand on her knee with a screech that not only hurt my ears but would also attract others' attention. I covered her mouth with one hand and kept it covered throughout the process. Turning my eyes to the left corner, a big shoulder-high portrait attracted my attention. It was of an old woman dressed all in grey; she wore a light grey dress, and the straps of the dark grey frock and cloth piece were wrapped around her neck. The old lady had her eyes wide open, staring towards me, as if in shock at what she was seeing. It brought a small laugh in my belly.

I could see that though the daughter of the old salesman was very young, almost seventeen, she wasn't a virgin. I don't know what other techniques she used to attract other guys, if she ever did, but I knew her techniques towards me. I also found out that many of the paintings on sale in her father's store were actually her own paintings. The funny thing was that I never got to know the girl's name; I didn't bother asking, and she didn't bother providing it free. Her father would just call her "daughter". I don't know whether to believe that the old man was really her father, as the age difference between them was very great.

On another occasion when I was in the city again, I took the chance to visit a local video store. When I asked for the English movie *There Will Be Blood*, the girl, being very busy tallying something on the counter desk, called her assistant. The assistant, Anh, started her welcome with a strange smile that followed a while of pause and gaze. I asked her for the movie, and she asked me to follow her. She wore a tight black T-shirt bearing at the back the name of the shop in yellow text. Her collars were apart with all the three front buttons open, and this created a nice V-shape on her milky chest with the point of the V falling into the darkness of the narrow space between her breasts. Her black pants seemed to me to be intended for sportswear, as its material didn't seem to be for an official use; it was fairly thin. She stopped at a rack and kneeled down. About twenty per cent of her concealed butt was visible, revealing the yellow T-back panties she had on, and the colour combination of black and yellow gave everything some boldness. Her curled brown-red shoulder length hair smelled of peach. I didn't know what she used for it, but it smelled fantastic. She stood up straight and handed me the DVD.

"You can rent anything here," she said and winked. The fake eyelashes did not suit her face.

Then she turned back and rested her body on the balls of her feet, sitting adjacent to the rack arranging some tapes. The big attraction in this scene was again her bottom; now almost half the butt was stretching out of the pants. With this delicious scene, I took the necessary pace towards her and slid my finger across the yellow line half the way in and drilled it where it first fitted.

Instead of getting the expected reactions, I got an unexpected one—a light giggle. But that was the appetite-opening serve, and everything with her followed next. I enjoyed her on the bed. She was sweet and professional, but she wasn't free. As she said before, I rented her every time I needed her. Who would mind paying for that beauty!

Trinh had always been a very good girl and a good example of a straight girl. This was what made me share a room with her for the first year and three months of my stay in Vietnam without having intercourse with her. She was a religious person, and sometimes when I went out with her, she would take me to some temples and even to churches. She said that she believed in one God and that whatever religion one follows, it will lead to the same God, the God of love and forgiveness.

I used to enter those religious places with her and see people doing their rituals towards whatever they believed might make them closer to God. I admit my heart was touched with some sacred feelings, and a stronger river of sorrow would flow in me. Those feelings would bring back questions about God and the purpose of believing in something, like being always with God. If I had ever been heartless, I turned so because of God. If I had been a lustful person for sex, I had been so because of Him.

What would you do when you have lost the grip on your life and when you see and feel only death? I am a man with my own path to follow. I am Godless.

One dark night, Trinh and I dragged an almost broken blue wooden bench with a back rest into the bushes miles away from our cottage. I recall it was a cloudy night. Far in the east, there was mute lightning emerging from time to time with a weak warning about any rain that might be expected. In the west, a half moon looked down towards us through a hole in the dark clouds that seemed to be specially made for it. The weather was mild, with gentle winds floating in between unmeasured intervals. A few grasshoppers were jumping in the grass, and we could only sense their presence when they leaped. Some rested on my feet for a while and tickled the veins there.

Trinh started talking about God, but I stopped her there asking her to change the subject. She talked about her family. Her father was a very devoted man in what he believed, but though having two girls, Trinh and her younger sister, her parents never got married because of some conflict between the two families that dated to almost fifty years ago. Her father was a fairly rich man, as she said. He owned farms and houses. His quest to make peace between the two families was always rejected, and his wish for marriage remained hanging as just a hope. That hope came to a dead end when the woman was killed in a road accident. The father's mind now turned to a determination to obtain the corpse of the woman of his life. The family of the woman made an impossible condition for him to satisfy his wish—to pay his entire wealth. The man made it all possible, and he got the corpse in the end, but now he had nothing to live on. Yet the new poverty didn't kill the man, but that sorrow of love did. Trinh worked different sorts of jobs for the sake of supporting her younger sister. When the younger sister opened her eyes more to the world around her, she chose a new and easy path of life—to be a sex worker. She left Trinh, but she never forgot her older sister; she kept sending her money every month, telling her that she wished to repay all the good things Trinh had done for her. That was how Trinh managed to obtain her college degree.

That night I found out for the first time that Trinh had already got a job in the city and she was to start in a couple of weeks.

She started moving her bottom on the bench then to the left and right and laughing, saying that she wanted to test the strength of it. I warned her that it was going to crack, but she refused to listen to me. It did break down in the end; the two back legs cracked. We fell on our backs, but her laughter continued forcing me to laugh as well. It all ended all in a couple of minutes, and we were now looking up at the black sky. The lightning increased its frequency, but it was mute as if the sky wished to listen to our little talk.

"Do you know why I used to colour my face at college?" she asked.

"No, but I wish to know," I replied.

"I am a virgin. I promised myself that I will lose this virginity only to the person I believe in."

"And when are you going to find that person?"

She turned her face to me, and at that moment a drop of rain bounced directly into my eye. Suddenly, the quiet sky spoke, and it spoke loudly. We collected ourselves and ran to our cottage. She was laughing again and leaping all the way. By the time we were there, our bodies were dripping wet. She brought in towels, and we started to dry ourselves. My eyes fell on her small chest, and for the first time I caught sight of those two nipples bumping through her wet dress. I raised my eyes to her face and could read in her face that she had already noticed my attention to those two small balls.

Without a warning, she pushed herself towards me, and her small wet lips were sucking mine. I caught her head with both my hands and pushed it back. A thin thread of mixed saliva hung low connecting both our mouths, but it broke fast. I looked her in the eyes.

"I am not the man you should believe in," I said seriously.

"You are just someone with a disturbed heart," she whispered. "I can see your true colours. I can sense your pure spirit."

She unlaced the threads at the front of her light yellow dress and with my support the dress was removed. I undressed myself, and she removed whatever parts she still had on. She came closer and our feet touched, her small feet in between mine. I flattened my lips against her rosemary-smelling neck.

I wouldn't disturb her virginity, you see. However bad I was and am, I wished her to give her purity to someone worthy, and I wasn't that person. Any feelings I had carried for her earlier fell there at that moment. With pure lust I approached her. Our wet flesh rubbed against each other, and her hard nipples pierced below mine.

I moved my face down and knelt on the ground. I gently caressed her thighs and opened them wide, and the secret of the moment was there. I started it there and ended it all there. I pushed my mouth hard there, and my wet tongue did the rest of the magic tricks. I kept licking her hard and eating her up. Being a girl inexperienced in the whole process, her whole body trembled and started shaking violently just at the first couple of minutes. I could see her face grow red and full of agonized pleasure. At first she put one hand on her mouth in an attempt to conceal whatever she was too shy to let out, but as the minutes passed, she gave up on that attempt, and I could see her now trying to keep up on her feet. Her moans were loud enough to increase my pleasure. Her arms spread and attached on each side onto whatever might have served as a support. It was nice hearing her scream for the first time. It was nice seeing her explode at the end and break down with weak legs.

I gave her the pleasure she might have sought. I just shook that nice rose; I didn't crush it.

At the end of my journey there, she gave me the following words:

"Unless you kill your sadness, you will die of it."

19

*O*nce I grew bored of my stay in Vietnam, I was to fulfil my promise to Howin, my college programming teacher. I returned to China and had only to show my face to Howin to get a job in the college I graduated from. Even so long after my graduation, I could see my affect still lingered on her. I believe the charms of my youth hadn't lost their captive power over her.

Soon after joining the college as a faculty member, I starting fucking Howin. I guess it was the reason she asked me to work there and was still accepting me. The woman was very proud of what she was getting in bed, and she started talking to other female faculty members about it. As a result of this, many middle-aged women in the college turned desiring eyes on me. Out of all of them, I allowed myself to enter the realms of only three in addition to Howin. I realized that most of them were already married and had kids, but I did what I was attracted to. The three I had chosen carried some sort of encouraging beauty in bed.

I was really upset to see those married women letting themselves loose for a desire that lasts only moments. The truth is that none of those women, including Howin, could hold it in if the intercourse lasted more than half an hour. I fucked them really hard with some anger, but that attracted me towards them even more. They had conscious unfulfilled desires that they wished to outsource to some temporary active partner, and a young one for sure.

It was the power of youth, the purely unconcealed influence in the eyes of those who have let much of it pass by and yet long to have it remain present in their lives. It was the fake sense of captivating beauty and charms of an age where everything may turn possible. It was the caprice of having a muscular manhood present in bed who can demonstrate in them the secret sexual whims that linger in their minds when their actual spouse has turned weak.

One of my female students, Li Chou, I admired. She always wore a short-sleeved white blouse and a long light-pink skirt, with the blouse tucked inside the skirt, whose belt rose up just a few inches below her chest. She was very tidy in her dress, the way she walked and spoke. She was a good student in programming and other subjects as well, as I was informed by other teachers. Though there had been eye-to-eye communications between me and her surpassing just respect, I didn't allow it to go any further. In the end I was a teacher, and carrying on with students might bring a bad reputation to the college.

To be a teacher didn't require me to gain any additional skill; all it needed was knowledge in what I talked about and confidence. I had enough of both, and so I was good at what I was doing. I didn't like the way Howin used to teach. I tried to make programming a delicious subject to my students, first because I liked programming, and second because I was getting paid for my job.

I wasn't satisfied though with only that job in hand. My mind was getting lost in the second half of the day when I sat alone in my apartment or in some coffee shop. Through readings and writings I used to do, I was getting depressed from time to time, sometimes very deeply. I was still some years away from my planned death schedule, and I didn't wish to end it there and then.

I stopped going to the free college gym, when one day I went to some local gym near my apartment and met my old friend, Bojing, who was now working there as a trainer. From then on, I used to attend that gym, for the first week as a trainee and after that as a trainer. Bojing gave the management there a good reference for me. I got some fitness tests and passed them all.

Bojing kept his body as fit as when we had worked out together in the college gym. It was as if he didn't increase or decrease any inch of muscle. Working with him gave me some fun. If there was one gay who acted "manly", that was Bojing. My part-time work in the gym was interesting.

Some nights he would take me to a bar. On our first encounter, he introduced me to a man as muscular as he was, with a thin face that didn't hide its physical moisturized beauty. After a while sitting together and exchanging casual chat, a creamy light-brown skinned girl approached the guy and sat just next to him on the long sofa opposite my small round seat. The girl had big eyes. I realized the skin colour of that girl was an adopted one. Her hair was blond, dyed just to fit the colour of the skin. After exchanging some secret codes with the guy, the new girl walked towards me like a model on a catwalk, pushed a seat next to me, and rested her artificially enlarged bottom there.

The girl rested her long-nailed hand and rubbed it between my thighs. I looked at the girl and smiled. My enjoyment of that caressing diminished within me when I turned my eyes to see Bojing and his friend sharing a light lip-to-lip kiss. I could discern then the sort of relationship between them. Just the thought of trying to imagine sexual behaviour between them brought sickness to my stomach. I turned my eyes back to the girl next to me to avoid the vomiting force that was growing within me.

"Come, our rooms are ready," Bojing's friend said to me. "The girl is booked for you for the night."

The two guys stood up, and I stood as well with my hand in the dry armpit area of the girl.

"You should eat well first," Bojing told me.

That night I hadn't eaten at all because I had been occupied with my busy training schedule for the day.

Bojing looked at his partner and they both laughed.

"You will need all you energy tonight," the partner added. Then he took a tiny bottle from his leather jacket's pocket and reached his hand in front of me. "Take this."

The light-yellow liquid in the bottle made me think of urine. I was already disgusted. I refused the offer and told them that I was going to manage the night just fine. I followed them then to the top of the stairs and to the row of rooms. They took the left one and I the right.

That night ended with me fully out of fuel. They were right; I needed all my energy, but I lacked it. I guess the girl was in her mid-twenties, and despite the softness she had shown earlier, she was really hard and capable of absorbing everything that matters. She left me dried out, and I left her unsatisfied. She left the room very upset and shouted in my face that I was as gay as my other two companions. That was the joke of the night back down in the bar with Bojing and his partner.

A month before leaving China, I opened my mail box. There were four letters, one from Qiuyue and the rest from Elizabeth, my uncle's wife. I started with the earliest dated, Qiuyue's letter.

> Thank you very much for the joys you spilled in my heart. I really and heartily appreciate all the good times you have spent with me. You are really a bliss for any girl that may come across your path.
>
> Sorry if I have left you without a single word. The truth is that I am bound to someone I am deeply in love with.
>
> I am going in search for a promised union.
>
> Faithfully,
> Q.

Her handwriting was as childish as her character. She might have been thinking that she left me broken-hearted and that I was in love with her. The poor girl didn't realize that I knew the story of her pathetic life fantasies and that I didn't love her at all. She didn't also know that her mother gave me more delicious pleasure than she did.

I opened the first two letters from Elizabeth. She wrote describing the bad medical situation of my uncle—that he was in the hospital and always vomiting blood. His health was declining day by day, she said, and he was continuously asking about me. Elizabeth mentioned that my uncle was in the last stages of his life, and she pleaded with me to come back and visit him for one last time to bring some happiness in his heart.

The last letter carried the unwanted news.

Your uncle died last week, and at the end the only thing on his tongue was your name. There were tears in his eyes as he called, not mine, but your name, turning his eyes to the left and right looking for you. But you were nowhere near us for the moment that most mattered.

I have seen children take shelter under a good falling roof. When they grow, they rebuilt the roof because of the simple protection it had offered them once in their life time. I have known young girls who have sold themselves for the sake of repaying the good deeds of their mothers towards them. I have heard of criminals changing to priests because of few touching words someone spoke to them in a polite way.

Years ago I took an evil into my home. I fed the child love while all it needed was hatred. When the whole world had abandoned him, my husband and I sheltered him. When he grew up, he simply abandoned us. That evil is you.

We gave you more care than your stupid mother had ever offered you. But you are a selfish, unfeeling man. My home shall ever remain closed for you. There is nothing ever between people who say nothing and never meet. I guess you have inherited nothing from your father but all the foolishness of your mother. God help your soul.

I still keep all those letters. It never pleased me to hear the news of the death of my uncle. I really loved him and respected him. It was true that I got the news late, but even if I had been informed of it earlier, I would not have gone back to the United States to visit him. As I mentioned earlier, I didn't wish to attach myself closely to anything or anyone. I believed it was better being away from others; living and dying with a free unbound heart.

I never blamed Elizabeth for carrying hard feelings against me. She might be right about them. Yes, it is true that I am an evil, but I never wished or planned to hurt intentionally anyone who didn't hurt me. For my part, I still and will always love Elizabeth and my uncle. I don't deny their good deeds bestowed upon me.

My visit to China had lasted two years and one month, but it ended there. I turned in my resignation at the college a month earlier. This time Howin didn't try to stop me from leaving. Having satisfied her whims with me, what more would such a woman require from me?

I left China with the sadness about my uncle and one sweet kiss at the end of my lips. That kiss was a gift from my student, the cunning Li.

20

$\mathcal{M}$y next ten months were spent in the Philippines, the country where heart-stopping scenery is mixed with poverty and where modern lifestyles are surrounded by primitive ones where even good food and shelter are lacking.

The first thing I did when I reached Manila was to buy myself a new guitar. It had been some time since I had last played on it, and I missed it. I found a simple crowded restaurant and took a seat. The bamboo-made restaurant was located on a narrow two-lane road, and the space separating the restaurant from the road was a small grassy slope. I wondered how that restaurant survived during the times of heavy rains that the country is used to.

The crowded restaurant was very quiet. It was as if all the people there had lost their tongues. Most of them were drinking liquors in small amounts, but none were speaking to the others. I turned my eyes around and caught some peaceful eyes fixed on me. The waiter approached me with a menu in hand. Giving a quick look at it, I ordered Halo-Halo.

"Don't worry about this people," the tender said in broken English. "They have his own problems."

The old men really looked sad, and the cracked lines on their faces were more than those on the rough tables of the restaurant. Most of them were looking out at the view of the sunset. The horizon was flaming in dark orange, and just the head of the sun was sneaking a look over the top of the humps of the mountains. That view might have brought some beauty to their inner selves as it brought into mine.

The waiter came back with a bowl of Halo-Halo in one hand and a spoon wrapped in a piece of tissue in the other. I paid for the order. I took my guitar and started with a low rhythm playing and singing:

> Jenny kissed me when we met,
> Jumping from the chair she sat in;
> Time, you thief, who love to get
> Sweets into your list, put that in!
> Say I'm weary, say I'm sad,
> Say that health and wealth have missed me,
> Say I'm growing old, but add,
> Jenny kissed me.[1]

[1] "Jenny kissed me" by Leigh Hunt

It was as if my music added lively souls to the half-dead bodies sitting on the cracked wooden chairs. They just started, though slowly, talking to each other and even smiling. I kept playing my guitar for the sake of seeing more of those old moving lips. Though their smiles added more wrinkles to their faces, they looked good wearing their smiles. I looked at the waiter, and he raised his eyebrows.

Suddenly, I saw a young girl walking towards my table. The next thing I saw was her hand stretched out holding a small card and then putting it on the table in front of me. I explored her face first before exploring the card. She had very short hair like a boy's that gave an overall fine look to her tiny skull, where the cheekbones were clearly visible and the eyes were slightly swollen, with the left one naturally narrower than the other. She had thin lips that matched well her skinny body. She looked just fair in my judgment.

I turned my eyes then to the card in front of me.

Hi, I am a student and I am in lack of money for my studies. I am selling peach sweets to support myself. One sweet pack for 50 pesos. Three sweet packs for 130 pesos. It will be a great help for me if you can buy some.

I looked up again but she was not there. I was willing to offer a hand of support. I put my hand in my pocket and took out 130 pesos. With my light mood at the time, I decided to make a small dirty joke with that young girl since I might not see her again. I took a pen from my other pocket and added at the bottom of the card, "130 pesos for 3 packs. How much to taste you for a night?"

I put the money on top of the card and I was shocked to see her suddenly standing in front of my table again. It was as if she could appear and reappear from nowhere. She picked up the card and the money, and looking just at the money, she withdrew three sweet packs from her long colourful shoulder bag. She thanked me, bowing her head, and then walked away. I fixed my eyes on her to see where she would be disappearing to. After taking a few steps away from me, she just vanished as the waiter walked past in front of me with a new customer. These two persons blocked my view for about two seconds, but the girl vanished within those two seconds. It reminded me of some magic show.

I remember that in my mind I was sure she would laugh when she read that card, or she would be embarrassed when she presented that card again to another person. I finished my Halo-Halo, took my guitar, and started playing again. I gave another turn of my head to find that skinny ghostly creature once again in front of me. I looked down where her eyes pointed and could make out those small digits after my handwritten question. They read "1000P".

So unexpected but so welcome! I paid her in advance before leaving the restaurant. I had her for the night, and she savoured it. She was as cheap and sweet as the peach candies she was selling. She asked me whether I was an artist or an actor. I said no. She told me that I looked like an actor.

About her, I just knew her name, Joseline, her age, twenty-two, the nature of her studies, marketing, and that she had represented some local shampoo brand a few years ago when she used to be less skinny and more handsome, as she explained. She suggested that if I would like to appear in some posters for a new brand of jeans, they would pay me fairly for it.

The idea sounded fine to me. A couple of days later she introduced me to the lady responsible for the promotion of the product, and I was accepted instantly as the model, after she had examined my top naked body closely with her eyes. The thing Joseline didn't tell me was that she would be getting paid commission for bringing me. I guess she didn't do a thing in her life for free, but that didn't matter to me. I got paid well for my topless pictures with the jeans pants that really didn't give me any comfort having them on.

I had casual sex one more time with Joseline, and this time I paid for her tuition for the whole year. She said that I was a noble man, but what nobility is there in feeding your lust upon someone young while paying for it? The important point she mentioned was that I could have her for any night I wanted, provided that she wasn't having exams. How interesting!

After my last session of picture shooting, I took one of those tricycles that can carry five to six passengers to my hotel. Riding in the front seat, I liked to see the view through the tiny front window and the side open. There was a small shoe hanging on the rear mirror by its lace, and it aroused the curiosity of another customer, when she asked the driver about it. He said that it belonged to his first daughter.

Whenever the tricycle stopped to pick a new customer, I would see eyes on me, some in shock as if they had seen an alien. Some girls would call each other and point at me, whispering to each other some words that best remained between girls. All the seats were packed, and still the driver let one more on. A woman dressed in a green T-shirt hesitated for a couple of seconds staring at me, before she sat to ride next to me. The air flowing in danced with her half-wet hair, which kept brushing against my face. It didn't bother me for the reason that its cinnamon smell cherished my nose and covered the smoky-smelling air that was hanging around.

I was the last customer left in the tricycle and was looking at the landmarks around me, and we were only a short distance from my hotel. But then a medium-sized white truck appeared in front of us speeding fast. There were a few wood boxes on the back of the truck, but nothing attracted my attention to it more than a mermaid creature who was sitting on top of one of those boxes in the middle of the open back of the truck.

I may not see that fascinating picture in my dreams, but I was lucky to see it in reality. How magnificent an artist coincidence can be! The girl was dressed in white with two floral layers attached at the end of each shoulder. The sunlight was very bright at the time, as I recall, and yet that girl sat calmly with the hot rays splashing her brown creamy skin. Her beautiful black hair was set flat on one side of her forehead, and her ponytail appeared on top of one of her shoulders. Her half-sleepy eyes looked deep into me.

I asked the tricycle driver to follow that truck. Why? I don't know. How? Mostly by signals rather than words. I put my hand in my pocket and brought out notes and put them scrambled in his hand. Giving them a quick glance, the big-chinned driver sped to follow the truck, and with the new speed, the small shoe swung hard. I had to move my head to one side to avoid it hitting me. The truck led us to a small cottage surrounded by skinny cows.

The truck stopped, and so did my tricycle. The truck driver got out and so did I, but concealing myself. The mermaid girl jumped off the truck into the tall grass. My eyes, searching for details, caught the outline of her light red panties from under that white skirt as she performed the jump.

The truck driver, a round-bellied man, walked towards the cottage, but his feet were not balancing properly on the ground. I figured out that he was drunk—at that early hour of the day! And how could he drive so well in that condition?

The girl struggled to push the wooden boxes out of the truck. She couldn't manage even a single box. Finding her alone, I walked up to her and offered a hand of support. Actually, I picked up the box that she had pushed to the edge of the truck and placed it on the ground. The girl looked at me with eyes full of worldly fear. Then she came nearer and pushed me with her light hands, murmuring something while shaking her head. Her hair was working like a spinning umbrella.

I couldn't understand her, and I was about to leave when the fat guy reappeared back from the cottage. His bald scalp bore tiny hair buds, and like a frog, his neck was invisible, but in his case it was due to the multi-layered packs of fat. His belly was so big that it made me wonder how he managed to have sex, if ever he did. His grim angry face, with a star tattoo on one jaw near the ear lobe, reminded me of some criminals I had seen on the National Geographic channel.

This fat balloon saw me with the girl, and he started shouting, turning his eyes from me to the girl. I believe he was throwing out some insults and bad words for both of us. Then he walked towards me, but the girl rushed to him pleading. The man slapped her and then, with his short legs, walked back to the cottage. I walked up to the girl and lifted her up, but with tears in her eyes, she screamed in my face. The right side of her pretty face was reddened.

Though the whole scene had been brutal, I thought it was I who had created the whole issue for the family, and so I started walking away with my back towards the drama. But as I took a few steps, I heard a louder quarrel, and another voice was added to the scene. I stopped and looked back to see the fat man, now carrying a butcher's knife and slowly walking, like a turtle, towards the weeping angel girl, with a woman hanging on to that fat hand of his, weeping as well.

I believed that things were getting worse there and it would be better if I didn't keep out of things. I started walking back to that group of three without being noticed.

He had thrown the middle-aged woman to the ground with a real punch and was now holding the butcher's knife raised in his hand to slash the girl. At that moment, my heart fell, and I saw myself running fast to stop my father slaying my mother, as they appeared in my mind's image.

My hand grabbed his hand that was carrying the knife. He turned his red bull eyes on me and landed a hard punch on my cheek that pushed me to withdraw a few steps. I raised my eyes and now it was just the image of that fat man that filled the landscape of my wrath. I didn't see my father any more.

Strangely, the man didn't approach me. Instead he moved again to the woman on the ground, who was clutching at the long grass with one hand. He raised his knife again, and only then did I put a stop to the whole play. I punched him hard on the centre of his flat nose. The giant ball-like figure fell to the ground with me on top of him. I started hammering his face with my fists. I was in a trance of mad anger.

In the end my body was grabbed by four hands, but this wouldn't have kept me away from my target had I not decided to back off because of the sad sound of female weeping. I was gasping hard, looking at the man on the ground with his face covered in blood. The girl kept weeping and screaming in my face. The lady embraced her and soothed her. Finally, the volume of the weeping decreased. The fat octopus on the ground crawled on his four limbs and then ran away as fast as he could, leaving behind two yellow teeth on the ground attached together by a string of loose bloody saliva.

The girl, Jemil as I found out later, was the woman's daughter. The mother could at least talk to me in English-Tagalog words, from which I could pick out the English words and build sentences in my mind. Jemil couldn't speak a single word of English, or it might have just been her feeling of embarrassment about speaking in broken English.

The mother invited me into the cottage and asked the daughter to prepare a cup of coffee for me. She explained that her husband had died long ago and that the fat man was the brother of her good husband. Though he was always drunk and was always beating the mother and daughter and sometimes even raping the mother, the fat man was supporting them financially. The fat man's business was to transfer wine from supplier to customer. The mother wasn't allowed to work, and Jemil was forced to accompany that drunk on his trips. The mother didn't hide from me that Jemil was even being offered to some rich men in exchange for cash, but the mother had to endure it all because of her fear of that fat man, especially after he had killed a young man who approached Jemil near the cottage and buried the body miles away.

My black coffee came, and Jemil sat next to her mother. Their two faces had similarities, except for the age lines and grey hair of the mother. I sipped the coffee with my eyes slyly settling on the beautiful Jemil, who continuously wiped her flattened hair to one side of her forehead with the bottom of her palm. Her hair was already laying nicely on the front of her head hiding the end of one eyebrow, but it was that unconscious motion that made that beautiful creature even more attractive.

The bitter coffee bit the front of my tongue. I listened to the mother worry that the fat man might come back and murder her and her daughter. I was sure that Jemil couldn't understand most of what her mother was saying, but the mother's nervous lips and eyes led the daughter to wrap her arm around her mother's shoulder.

The light-brown dry skin of Jemil enchanted me. I wished to see her again and again the same way, with her skin gleaming under the slightest spark of light and wearing the same angel-like white dress, but that wish didn't come true. I offered the mother and daughter enough money to go away and start a new decent life. The mother whispered to me, asking whether I wished to be their companion and marry her daughter. My first question to her was whether Jemil's heart was free. The answer was that it was already secretly attached to a decent young farmer. We agreed to separate, but my heart was aching; I had not received even a single kiss from Jemil.

I wouldn't have married Jemil even if her heart hadn't belonged to someone else, and I wouldn't have hurt or cheated her to get my desire satisfied. It was just my eyes that craved having her, not my heartless heart. What a shame it was, I thought, that Jemil and I couldn't commune with each other due to language differences. What a shame that fate didn't put her in my bed. But what a decent girl she was! I wished to frame in my mind the innocent smile she gave me the moment we separated. It was a real hearty way of saying thank you.

21

$\mathcal{T}$he last thing I did in the Philippines was to learn the craft of cross-stitching. Though it might seem a girlish hobby, it was art nonetheless, and arts extend throughout cultures and genders. I had seen expensive stitched pictures and I enjoyed gazing at their details, but up to that point I had never decided to learn it.

I had come across the new line as I was roaming in a small local shopping mall. I remember seeing a European guy walking beside a local Filipina girl, and at one point his hand moved from her shoulder down to her ass, where he placed a few gentle pats. He was a good hungry man like me at the time.

Hidden between two big stores, one for hardware and the other for home appliances, there was a tiny store for cross-stitching that offered patterns, threads, and also big expensive ready-made portraits. Some girls and old women, but not a single man, were busy buying, until I approached, at which point all eyes were fixed on me, except for those of one lady who pushed others aside as she drilled her way forward to pick up what she liked.

The crowd of females split apart to give me access, as if I was some sort of a special character (which I didn't wish to be).

Ignoring the murmuring crowd, I examined the different pictures available for sale. I liked a picture of greenery with waterfalls and one of a sitting baby girl wearing her diapers. One attractive picture showed a nude lady in a seductive pose. It was that picture I was holding when I heard a soft voice.

"I see you have an artistic taste."

I raised my head to see a reddish-brown short-haired, oily-skinned face. The smile showed straight white teeth. A good-looking girl, I told myself. The next thing I wished to see was the chest size. There, my eyes got lost searching for any sign of even immature breasts inside that tight light—and dark-pink striped shirt. But there was nothing more than a flat chest. Then I realized that I was looking at a gay man!

"Do you like stitching, sir?" he asked.

"I don't know how to stitch," I replied, and I was preparing myself to leave now. I put back in the basket the picture I was holding.

"Perhaps you would like to learn how to stitch if you can afford to pay," he said.

I paused and hesitated, thinking about his offer and what side effects might arise as part of that deal. He was a gay, and a very proud one, I saw.

"Okay," I agreed.

"Does it always take you so much time to come up with an answer?" he asked and then continued. "Decisions are to be made in a split second, and that is what makes some more unique than others."

I thought about how he was so unique and different from the men and women around him. He pushed his head towards me then, and in an instant reaction, my head pulled back a few inches. His shampooed hair smelled good in its herbal flavour.

"You will be safe with me. I am not intending to hit on you. I have a boyfriend."

That was very thoughtful of him and very relaxing for me to hear. He took my phone number and gave me his and told me that he was going to call me by the next day. We separated, and I went back to my apartment, where I read for a couple of hours and lost track of time. By the evening, my stomach had started generating a sort of noise that suggests I should go on a hunt for food. I dressed and left.

I ended up eating duck products—meat and egg. It was the first time I had ever eaten duck, and it was delicious. I was licking my fingers, when a group of fine-looking young men started walking quickly out of the dimly-lit restaurant I was in. Throwing a quick glance on them, I focused back on my table. But one of them stopped at my table. Not knowing any of them and not having any interest in doing so, I didn't raise up my head, but my fist tightened into a defensive preparation for whatever unexpected bad behaviour might arise.

"Your pockets seem to be full," the young man said.

I looked at him now and raised my eyebrows. His creamy round-brimmed hat was leaning on one side of his head.

"They say tonight they are holding some tits competition over in the bar."

The idea sounded intriguing, vague though it was. Just hearing that suggestion raised my spirits a little.

"Would you like to join us?" he asked.

The guy looked over at his other three friends; all were wearing caps and all had them pulled to one side. They were waving at him, asking him to hurry. I left my chair and joined them.

I think we looked good together, me and that band of four. To make it look even better, I excused myself near a shop and went in and bought myself a hat similar to the ones they had on, and I pulled it down on the left side of my head. I think it brought me closer to my crazy new colleagues. One of them offered me a drink he was holding in his hand and sipping from time to time. Believing it to be some strong wine, I closed my eyes before taking a big sip. But what a ridiculous joke! It was just a soft drink—Mountain Dew, I guess. I looked at them, and they laughed at me.

"We don't drink, you see," one of them said.

"But we like to have adventures," the other added.

"I see," I commented.

What adventures they had, being afraid to fall under the influence of alcohol!

They stopped in front of a small room where cheap colourful lights were hanging from the roof like a wedding, dangling in small curves. It was like some fairy room in a children's bed-time story, where a short funny-faced evil old woman lives quietly, waiting for her victim, which must be a child. The noise inside started getting louder and louder, and the young group I was with rushed in through the narrow door-less opening that was covered with a blanket.

The competition was to start shortly, and I could see some topless girls. My group dug their way through the crowded bar, and I followed their trail. While trying to avoid any physical contact with anyone there, I let my hands loosely brush the sweaty hips and thighs of the cute females in the crowd. How strange that so many girls would attend a competition that was for the same gender as them! Most men would feel embarrassed or disgusted to stand in front of another man and stare at his private parts, but all those girls were chanting and enjoying themselves looking at other half-naked females. Women have more privileges than men, it seems.

I didn't have to push a single person to reach the front line; my group had special access because of the bright image they showed of themselves. People are always aware of status and the threats it may present.

Four girls and one woman sat on square white plastic chairs, stripped of their bras. The tits, of different sizes, exposed their nipples into the semi-damp atmosphere, and they were enjoying the chattering of the herd and bringing joy into the unlawful joy-seeking hearts. I was, of course, one of that herd; I wasn't much better than any of them, if I was any better at all.

A black-teethed thin guy with narrow red eyes approached the first line of attendees and walked around the girls' breasts waiting for the start of the competition. He reached his hands up, and I could feel him standing on his toes to push himself a little higher than his normal height, and the dusty brownish flesh of his belly fell out, sneaking onto the brown belt that was wrapped around the modern-style shredded jeans that were decorated by the natural age of the cloth. But the thing to mention about the guy is that he didn't smell at all bad. He posted a hand-written A—size piece of paper on a few pillars that were fully covered with advertisements.

I raised my head, and so did my league, and we looked at the new post, "Rules of Competition," it said in big text, and below it were the points.

Band Size Measurements Plus 5 inches
Cup Size measurement
Regular Bra Size

And below these lines, there was a note that read, "Free 750ml beverage for the winner". Then I lowered my eyes and saw the thin guy placing a Tanduay bottle on top of the wooden box that contained music speakers. A bottle of rum! I thought I just couldn't see anything logical in getting such a cheap prize in a competition where the females have to expose their private parts to the public. But there was really no logic in the whole of what was going on there, and that made that particular competition even more fun.

A new character was introduced then to the scene—a crude-looking girl in her late twenties with red-brown highlighted hair that was shorter than mine. Her yellowish eyes made her look like someone addicted to some illegal drug. Her shoulders were stretched out, and they resembled those of a man. She appeared from the back of the competitors and, to amuse them, she walked past brushing her big fingers against their bare backs. She stood now in front of them and scanned them with her eyes. I could see she was a tomboy from the way she was looking at those girls.

The tomboy approached the first girl and quickly she wrapped around her chest the white measurement tape she carried in her pocket. She brought a small gasp from the girl by adding a little pull as she was holding the ends of the tape. She tightened the tape around the girl's ribcage directly under the bust and then released the tape and picked out a tiny pencil and a square piece of paper to write down the measurement. Again she wrapped the tape around the girl, but this time she laid it around the fullest part of her bust. She noted down the measurement again. Amidst a huge noise from the crowd, the tomboy moved to the next girl, and so on. I could see that she was savouring her work; anyone who has any elements of manhood would cherish the opportunity to caress different sizes of soft tits. She made a longer stop when she measured the last lady; I could find only one reason for that—the large dark areolas.

The tomboy went back for a minute and then returned to announce the winner. But just at that moment a young girl rushed in, pushing through the crowd and shouting. The noise of the crowd went a bit lower, and all eyes turned to the newcomer. The girl who had just arrived was the prettiest girl in the room, wearing tight light-blue shorts and a light-green T-shirt. Her hair was just touching her shoulders, but it was very thick like a lion's. She was gasping, and her perspiration was making damp spots through the T-shirt.

The young princess stood in front of the tomboy, whose jaw was as open as mine, and took off the T-shirt. The big jugs she carried on her chest fascinated the room, given her young figure, and the noise grew louder than ever. All those topless girls in the room didn't enchant me as much as she did. I think she enchanted every single man in the room. She had fairly white skin that loosely allowed a few red veins appear visible at the top of her thigh, and she had one green one along the surface of her throat. The yellow straps of her green bra struggled to hold the weight of her jugs. She reached her hands and unhooked the bra and there they jiggled, two human natural humps covered in moisture.

The tomboy stepped towards her, wrapped the measuring tape around her, and took all the necessary measurements. Putting the measuring tape into her pocket, the tomboy jokingly cupped one hand on the young pumped breast. The young girl, full of confidence, just looked in the eyes of the half-woman, and that was enough to push that hand away from her chest. The tomboy withdrew and, raising her voice, announced the winner. It was the new young girl. The tomboy proclaimed that her bra size was 36DD, and she was—no surprise—just fourteen years old.

I had a question in my mind of how they figured out the bra size, but as soon as the question started to linger in my mind, the guy who had asked me to join his colleagues came to my rescue.

"Do you know how they find the cup size?"

"No," I replied simply.

But my answer seemed to show my ignorance to the guy. He looked at the friend who was standing beside him, and they both smiled.

"They take first, as you saw, the band size, which is the measurement of the ribcage just under the bust. They add five inches to the measurement, and if the resulting value is an odd number, they go to the next even number. Then comes the cup-size measurement, and this is taken by measuring around the fullest part of the bust. The formula is to subtract the band size from the cup size. The regular bra size is determined based on this result; if one inch or less, then it is A cup, two inches is B, three is C, four is D, and five is DD."

I appreciated this excellent information from this very young man. I smiled at him and nodded to show my gratitude for the clarification.

Tanduay was presented to the winner, and the girls started putting on their dresses, and most of them were murmuring unhappily about the winner. The competition ended, and the crowd got busy drinking and dancing. Four sexy girls approached, and they happen to be attached to the group I accompanied. They exchanged kisses, and the boys shook hands with me before merging in the crowd with their girls, one of whom secretly looked back at me and sent me a flying kiss in the air.

But I remained in my place, standing and staring at that enchanting young girl, who now put on her bra and with a little force pulled back the straps to push up her tits. When she was done with the hook, she glanced at me but ignored me and picked her T-shirt, adjusting it by pulling it inside out, and slid her head through it so that when it came out of the top, her hair was bushy. She put her hands through it and brushed it out. Holding her Tanduay bottle, she looked at me again and came nearer.

"You have good eyes, sir, and a good nose," she commented.

"Only if you see them so," I said.

"You might want to invite me for a drink." She smiled.

"I thought alcohol is not legal at your age."

"Nor is it legal to have sex with an underage girl." She raised her thick eyebrows.

I guess she understood the ultimate meaning of our meeting. I invited her for a couple of drinks, as she wasn't satisfied with just one. In the middle of the drinks, I asked her about her family and how she managed to attend such a loud party, being so young. She told me that just two days ago her "dictator uncle", as she called him, had passed away and she was now free; that during the life of her uncle, who took care of her after the death of her parents, she was banned from drinking, partying, having a boyfriend, and even staying out late at night.

At the end of the conversation, she was very loose and her behaviour turned childish. What an unfaithful child she was. Just hearing what had earlier been taboo for her made me pity her poor uncle. How ungrateful and narrow-minded humans can be sometimes!

I gladly helped the girl stand and wrapped my arm around her under her bust. The tips of my fingers were free to feel the bottom elastic of her bra. Relentless haste was eating me and provoking my lust for that demandingly unique individual. I delivered her to my hotel room, where she started dancing around under the sweet influence of alcohol. I let her do whatever she liked in my green-painted room; she slightly collided with a small table and fell down and burst into hysterical laughter; she hit with her hand a hotel-owned flower vase and smashed it on the floor; she babbled words, many of which were bad ones.

I didn't care about all those extra rotten aspects on her bad surface character. I knew that she was going to lie in my bed in the end and that I cared about being with her that night. And that is what happened in the end. She jumped on me, really jumped, and I took few steps back to keep myself balanced on my feet. Her breasts pierced through my chest, but I wasn't satisfied with that. I picked her up under her bottom and had her sit on a foam-padded wooden chair. I stripped off her T-shirt and then put my fingers under the lower band of the front of her bra, while I lay the second hand just directly under the left breast. It was an intentional act to hold in my hand a sweet sensation. I loved to feel the wet weight of that full breast fall sweepingly and slide unto the surface of my palm. I held it and squeezed it gently like a lively flower and brushed my thumb around the light areola and atop that young nipple. I caressed that young beauty of the night, and the best part was when I went into her; that one green vein That ran along the side of her throat tightened, thickened, and popped out beautifully as her pupils turned up under her eyelids, leaving behind the white sclera like newly turning ghost.

The night went well, very well, as it the lustful demands of that soft beauty extended our spirit of pleasure. I don't know how many hours I slept in between feeding upon that juvenile vagina and skimming my cheeks against the soft god-sent beauties of that young chest.

Then my mobile phone rang—something that hadn't occurred for the last month or so. I opened my eyes slightly with my blurred vision and reached my hand to my left to feel for my mobile on the bed.

"Who is this?" I asked, answering the phone.

"This is John James," the voice replied.

I remained silent in my half-awake state, trying to figure out who the speaker was.

"The guy from the cross-stitching shop." The voice came as if reading my mind.

How could I not recognize his soft voice, but why should I? I rubbed my eyes with the bottom of my palm and saw that the digital wall clock read 6:05 a.m. I couldn't believe that I was getting a call from that strange guy at that early hour of the day. Then in a flash my mind recalled the big-breasted teenager I had slept with last night. With the phone held to my ear, I pushed up my body on the bed and looked next to me. There was only the scrambled bed sheet, the one part of the mess we created together, but she was nowhere to be seen. The room was very quiet, apart from the music that leaked out from the mobile phone. I flipped the bed sheet over and stepped out of the bed and peeked into the toilet, but there was no sign of her. One thing that jumped into my mind was whether I was dreaming about the joy of the previous night, but her yellow panties lay among the scrambled bed sheets.

"Can I meet you today?" John James said.

"Okaaay." I said blindly, while reaching down to the bed and picking up the panties with the tips of my fingers.

"I will see you then by five."

"Okay." Another unconscious reply came from me, and now I was examining the underwear in my hand and starting to believe the reality of the big-breasted princess in my bed. And on the floor there existed yet another proof—the shattered remains of the colourful flower vase.

All of a sudden I felt as if the eyes of John James were on my nude body as I stood near my bed. I pulled off the bed sheet and wrapped it around my waist with a single hand.

John James ended the call and only then did I realize the commitment I had given that guy. But two things were missing from my room: the girl and my wallet. She wasn't just an untamed badly behaved child; she was also a thief. But I guess she deserved the eight thousand pesos in the wallet; that wasn't a loss for me at all. There was nothing personal in the wallet, and I was one step wiser than I had been.

22

$\mathcal{I}$ started my training with John James that same day. From just standing and watching him work on the cross-stitch pattern, to sitting together in a restaurant, and finally to accepting his invitation to go and work in his home, we got to know each other well. He appeared to be interesting to talk with and a funny character, but my hidden internal objection was to him being gay. It is not that I have any prejudice against homosexuals; I believe that one should do what one believes in, and one shouldn't care much about what others do in the world as long as they mean no hatred or malice towards others. It is just that I always feel slightly uncomfortable around gays. Thus I was always somewhat hesitant in my dealings with him. I got some comfort seeing him answer his mobile phone on a regular basis and saying that it was his boyfriend. I didn't wish to mingle with such types; I have always been straight in my sexual tendencies.

Cross-stitching happened to be a very easy leisure-time task to learn. It required just one day to learn its techniques and one week to master it. My time with

John James was at an end, and I wished to pull myself away from him, but he suggested that we could work on a piece of art that would cost us nothing more than time and would bring us cash in our pockets. He almost pleaded with me, saying that if money wasn't important to me, it was to him and that he couldn't finish a big piece of work alone because he was always busy during the first half of the day at the shop, and in evenings he would feel lazy and too tired to do any extra job.

I agreed not because of the cash I would make out of that hobby, as I knew it wouldn't bring enough to feed me, but to help him fill his pocket. And so we started working on a 60 by 50 inch Aida canvas on a picture entitled "Green Life In Africa"; it showed the sun sending its rays over the colourful clothed heads of black happily smiling ladies enjoying their noon-time harvest. I wished the picture was applicable to real life.

It was really a tedious job to work on that picture. Initially, I started working on it in my apartment hour after hour just to rid myself of a wrongly made commitment. One day John James invited me to join him in his apartment, saying that he would help me with the picture. I had visited his apartment on previous occasions in the initial stages of learning, and so it didn't intimidate me to visit it again. It had been one whole sexless week for me, and the task was consuming my effort. I was feeling pain at the top of my shoulders from continuously sitting over the task with my head bent.

His apartment was so plain and clean. He hung stylish pictures of himself on different angles of the walls, made ugly with makeup and hairstyles that killed any little beauty he possessed. He asked me to sit and listen to him sing. I did what he asked, and he brought me a glass of wine. Sitting next to me on the purple rug, he pulled out his recording ornaments. I pushed myself aside before he could start his recorder and video camera and sing.

What a magnificent voice he had! His voice was no different from John Mayer singing "Say What It Needs to Say". Such a strange character possessed a magnificent voice. He finished his song and stopped recording himself. Then he dragged into the scene his Apple laptop and connected it to the net. Opening the YouTube website, he uploaded his recently taken video and then asked me to and watch a video. Despite the beauty of his voice, I wasn't keen to hear him sing the same song, but the video he showed me was a different one, and below it was in bold the number of times the song was watched, 3726, and a few comments were placed beneath the video.

I simply, without any wonderful words, congratulated him on his talent and asked whether we could work on our Green Life in Africa. I didn't wish to sit the whole evening with him. And so he turned his hand to the picture, and we started working together, me quiet and his lips trembling with some sort of local song. I could catch him glancing at me and the glass of wine I had placed next to me. He wanted the glass back, I thought, and so I swallowed its half-full contents in a single sip. As I vaguely recall, there was a foggy smile on his face afterwards, and in the midst of my clouded view, I could see him as an imaginary ghost approach me with a small pink digital camera, and the flash exploded into my eyes, blinding them.

When I opened my eyes, John James was sitting in front of me stitching. His dark-pink top dress brought some discomfort to my eyes. I found it surprising to find myself lying on the rug, unconscious of anything around me. I sat and rubbed my eyes and saw him still singing and working. He turned to me then.

"I see you were so tired you fell asleep here," he said.

"How long have I been sleeping?" I asked, still not believing myself.

"I guess one and a half hours." He sighed and leant back, resting his palms on the rug.

"It is nine-thirty," I said looking at the wall clock. "I think I need to go."

I stood and glanced at the empty glass of wine still set near my bare feet, and a big doubt came to my mind about the possibility that the wine was drugged. Otherwise I wouldn't have fallen asleep in such a strange home in the company of such a weird character.

"I would be pleased to introduce you to a friend of mine," he added, and I felt so deadly bored of him and his oracle-like attitude. "This sister of mine wishes to see you. I have been talking to her a lot about your gentle character."

Now my anger relaxed, and a beam of golden light emerged inside me. A girl, he mentioned, and I would be pleased to meet one. I had to conceal my sexual activities, even talking about them, in his presence. It had been almost two weeks since I had last encountered sex and pleased the beast inside me. I thought it was one more of his hidden tricks to play upon me, but I told myself that I wouldn't fall into being alarmed now by his weirdness.

I accepted his proposal, and we went out. He walked in the smelly darkness of the neighbourhood night like a girl, shaking his bottom while walking, which filled me with disgust. His dark pink dress flashed in the darkness and showed him even more, especially in his tight shiny black leather pants. The cracks in the asphalt of the road were filled with water, sewage I guess, and different coloured dogs strolled around peacefully, barking occasionally. A few unattended old men were walking to their destinations unnoticed and without causing the slightest distraction to anyone. One blind man held a stick as old as he was, and a child, covered with sand and dust, gripped the middle of the stick to guide the old man, while his eyes followed the people dining and joking around him and the children running after one another, laughing.

The humid atmosphere brought beads of sweat to my skin. I wiped with a single finger a drop of sweat from my eyebrow and splashed it on the ground. As I looked straight ahead now, there was a bunch of young people sitting on the pavement, sipping liquor and looking straight at us and laughing with some words that I couldn't understand. They meant nothing to me and my only option would have been to ignore if they hadn't said something else.

"Gay John got a handsome gay," one of those drinking cockroaches said.

I stopped, and anger boiled inside of me. I turned to that bunch of garbage of night.

"You got a problem, motherfucker?" I maintained a calm voice as I spoke.

They laughed, and I could see the whole group joking with the one who initially made that comment about me and encouraging him to take some action against me. The half-wet sweating guy stood and took a small knife from the man next to him, who had been cutting and swallowing a green apple a piece at a time. The guy approached me from the front, and so did John James from my back. I didn't feel safe with the gay anyway, and my initial thought was that it was all a part of a plan between John James and that young drunk bunch. I didn't care much about anything; there was no fear inside me, and I was an unfeeling creature. The guy pointed that small brown-handled knife in my face. I looked in his eyes for a while. There was a river of fear. With one hand I slapped his knife away, and with my other hand I gave him a half-strength punch on his cheek. I don't know whether it was the force of the punch or just acting that made him lie on the ground, but I do suspect that there was an element of the latter. His dirty group vomited out dirty unpleasing laughter. I looked at the guy on the ground and waited for any further action from him, but he stayed quiet. I believe his fear didn't allow him any more injection of ridiculous bravery.

"Let's go, let's . . . go, Gerald." John James pulled me by my hand, and I followed him.

I cooled down, but his hand was still resting on my arm, and I had to shake it off.

He knocked on a door with a Christian cross on it. It took some time for somebody to approach and look through the door peephole. Finally, the door opened in front of me and a young girl the colour of light chocolate was standing there with big eyes and thick lips.

"Hi, sister," John James said, and the girl asked us in, but before closing the door, she popped her head out and checked around. We sat on scratched out tiny round foam chairs and the girl sat on a small sofa bed.

There was a moment of quiet, and my eyes tested on the girl and her small room. Then I could see the girl looking at John James and nodding. I turned to the gay, and there was a smile on his face. The girl stood and went out to the tiny kitchen. I could see she was about to prepare some drink for me. Having learned a lesson from my earlier experience that night, I raised my voice and told her in rather a fierce tone that I was not in need of anything.

"Juice?" she said, and her eyes met John's again.

I shook my head, and she sat back on her sofa bed. Again the dreadful silence came back for a couple of minutes, and my whole thoughts was frankly hoping that John James would leave the room and leave me alone with that simple mysterious girl. The girl kept looking at John James from time to time in some sort of secret request.

"The sister wants to bed you," J. J. said.

I stared at him amazed. How bravely and easily he let that sentence out, as if asking for a simple favour or sharing a genuine thought. I was about to confirm the truth of his comment in her eyes, when I turned my face and a new symbol struck me—a medium-sized cross on the wall, below which were engraved the lines:

So do not fear, for I am with you.

Do not be dismayed, for I am your God.

Initially a huge doubt entered my mind about the girl being in some sort of church service, but reassurance came when I noticed a nun's black-and-white dress that she had failed to conceal among other long dresses hanging across the horizontal wall-hanger. A nun to taste! What surprises life brings upon us from sources where we expect nothing.

I looked at the girl, and her eyes suddenly shifted from me to John James. I could see the truth in his comment; she didn't deny anything, and she didn't seem to do want to do so with even a single expression. Her silence meant much to me; it gave me a warrant to arrest a servant of the church between my legs, permission to satisfy what I hadn't been able to satisfy for the last two deprived weeks. What purity the church workers seek when they are still self-slaved for their lust!

"Will you leave us alone?" I asked John.

"Who? Me?" John looked at the girl and then at me. He produced a laugh, the sort that is filled with surprise at hearing something funny. "No, I am staying here. I am just a guest you shouldn't worry about."

I looked at the girl, and she gave a slight wink with both her eyes, a sign of approval.

Who would care about having a pet in a room while having sex? I believed him to be harmless unless left unattended. Ignoring the identity of the girl and the fact that there was a third eye in the room, I walked to the girl and stroked her face with the back of my hand. She took a deep breath, and I sensed the nerves on her face on alert. It was the result of the poverty of the church in providing what the hidden self needs and slyly seeks. My inner self longed for the warm touch of bare breasts against my chest. Placing my hands atop her shoulders, I gently pushed her onto her sofa-bed and peeled off, piece by piece, the unnecessary burden that stood between me and the period of limited joy. Her clawless fingers scratched my back with hot pleasure that she might have been deprived of for a long time.

I guess she was hungrier than me and in shameless need of sex. Why else would a simple nice-looking girl like her abandon whatever self-respect she possessed and step upon her religious path with the disgrace of a single night. And what a disgrace it was to allow another human to watch her transgress her fake loyalty to God. Any normal girl wouldn't go as far as that girl, a servant of God. You sometimes get curious to learn more details about such widely spread creatures on earth, to know the reasons behind their wild deeds. But at that moment, I didn't. All I cared about was how to consume her to the fullest of my satisfaction and the extreme of her arousal.

I cleaned up my mess after me and wiped my genitals with the girl's panties. I turned now to see a strange smile on John's face. His eyes scanned certain parts of my body, which was covered with good-smelling perspiration that came from the girl lying asleep after being properly serviced and fed. I put on my clothes and walked out of the house.

"You see, all sinners are saints," J. J. said as he closed the door behind him and started walking with me.

I didn't reply. I stopped the first tricycle and went back to my hotel. That same night, I started planning to escape the country and that strange gay. I started feeling uncomfortable in his company. The next destination that struck me was Beirut, the capital of Lebanon. It came as an advertisement on the BBC news channel.

The next day John James called me and asked me to pick up the canvas from him to work on. Inside me I sighed, but I had given him my word and felt bound to fulfil it. I did pick up the canvas from his workplace and started working on it gain.

After a week or two of non-stop working on the portrait, there came gentle knocks on the door of my room. I didn't remember having ordered anything for dinner that evening. I opened the door, and John James came in uninvited with a rolled Aida canvas in one hand. That evening he had a shawl wrapped around his neck, and I wished to suffocate him with it.

"Your room looks nice," he commented, and his voice seemed softer than ever.

"How do you know where I live?" I questioned.

"People leave traces behind them. Collecting them may not be as hard as it seems."

Again he seemed mysterious, or he just acted so, but I hated that part of him more than any other. He stared at me then, and for the first time when our eyes met for a couple of seconds, he didn't lower his gaze. There was strange desire in them that I tried to turn off by turning my face away.

"So, why this sudden visit?" I asked.

"I got this for you," he replied, stretching his hand along his shoulder.

"What's this?" I said, and I took the rolled canvas from his hand.

I took a step or two away and rolled out the canvas. A wonderfully designed picture of my face was woven on the surface of that milky-coloured Aida canvas. It was so pleasing to look at the portrait, and it was a real piece of art. It was my face stitched on the canvas, so nicely and delicately. At the bottom corner of the picture J. J. had stitched his signature. Honestly speaking, I was so happy about it and I was ready to pay for it in cash even double what its real value might be.

I was about to turn to him and ask him its price, but then two hands were thrown lightly around my chest and a head was pressed against my back. I looked over my shoulder to see that gay pushing against me, and I could sense the surface of his penis pressed against the bottom of my ass.

"I love you, Ger," he said.

Ger! Since when had I had a nickname? He made up things based on his desires, I guess. A wet drop seeped through a spot at the back of my T-shirt to touch my skin; I could sense he was emotionally crying.

"I have always desired you." Now his nose was running.

I forced the bracelet-like hands around my chest to break apart, and I pushed that witch off my back. I fired a strong look at him. He was wiping his nose now with his black shawl. His tears made lines along his cheeks in a darker colour than the rest of his white-powdered face.

"Haven't you loved somebody in your life?" He unwrapped the shawl now and dropped it on the floor and took off his black long-sleeved top and dropped it too on the floor. His skinny body looked so plain and unmuscled that I thought he looked like a real catwalk model. "Will you fuck me the way you fucked my sister the other night? Embrace me like a tender flower and sway me in your arms."

As he started walking towards me, I slashed the canvas across his face, but though it hurt him, it didn't stop him. He continued to walk, and I gave him a hard angry slap on his face across his nose, which started bleeding immediately.

"Get out of my room, you freak," I shouted.

He stopped in shock and pain. I held him by his hair and neck and dragged him out and shut the door behind him. I picked up the canvas from the floor, opened the window, and threw it out. Immediately I packed up my bag and went online and booked my ticket for the next day morning. The ten month stay in the Philippines was over.

23

*I*n the Rmeil district of Beirut I sat with a small basket of coloured balloons and a balloon pump. I was twisting the balloons into different shapes. This was a new hobby that I worked on after learning from Internet resources for the last couple of days. I practiced mainly on the streets for the enjoyment of children, who would stop and look with joy at me twist the balloons, and they would buy some of the shapes from me.

The interesting part of practicing that hobby wasn't the presence of the young children, but the presence of white and creamy-skinned females with their short tight dresses. Even the old ladies had their faces coloured and their ears and hands embroidered with jewellery.

I had a piece of luck one Sunday on the street as I sat crafting my hobby when at mid-day a character started pacing quickly across my area of work, forcing me to shake my eyes along with the violent shakes of her mid-sized breasts. It was so amazing to look at those two dumplings on the surface of her chest jiggle in such a strange manner, given their normal size. My eyes were struck with the flash of the movements of this young blonde, a guest in the kingdom of my lust. I recall that at the moment I saw the girl I was working on a red teddy-bear balloon for a young boy who was standing by me. I just completely lost track of him and his presence. Who would be able to focus back on his work after noticing the vigorous tide of that human female?

My eyes narrowed, searching for the straps of her bra through the white shirt she had on, and I was more amazed when I found it. It still annoyed my head to think about those young breasts rebelling through the combined layer of shirt and bra. But that wasn't the only special thing about that girl, for apart from her young face, there was the special scent she spread in the air that refreshed the humid atmosphere of the street. Every eye turned in the direction of that scented deer, but I was more greedy than most.

I left everything behind and walked with the wind, having my nose and my curious lust as my guides. I started weaving my daydream with that girl, even without being sure that she would be part of the true strings of the portrait. I followed her, mainly walking steps away at her side and pleasing my poor eyes with the fast motion of the girl's two cups. At one point, she paused all of a sudden and gave me a quick gaze and a tiny smile, before continuing on her way. I realized that she knew that I was following her, and she simply allowed it for my ignorant gladness.

She stopped among some big houses and unlocked the small door of her house, which, compared to all those around it, seemed a veritable midget. Everything was decorated—from the green line of flowers in front, to the door and the doorsteps, to the light pink-white paint. She went inside the door and gave me one more look before closing the door.

I walked up to the door, and a rosy scent tickled my nose and welcomed me. I inhaled deeply and pressed the doorbell without thinking what I was doing. In a split second, the door was answered and one half of the bright moon was standing behind the half-open door. It was as if she was expecting a visitor.

"Yes?" she said in a tone that was more like a question.

"I . . ." I started, as I recall, but I didn't know how to go about it until her eyes fell on the teddy-bear balloon in my hands. I grasped the clue and built on it.

"Do you wish to buy this?" I spoke.

And then I realized how remarkably silly it was to speak those words in such circumstances. The silliness of that remark was mirrored in her face, and a smile appeared on her tiny red mouth. I could see now the blue of her eyes, oceanic and lovely. Two petite light-red patches embellished the white background at the top of her cheeks. She was very short, barely reaching my shoulders.

"How much for it?" She placed her hand on the head of the teddy bear.

I searched for an answer, and my eyes fell to the luxury of her bosom. I guess that was enough of an answer, because she asked me if I wished to come in and have a cup of tea. A cup of tea! I read it as a good sign to start with. Girls never ask you to come into their homes unless their inner selves yearn for something.

She walked in, but as I tried to step in after her, my forehead collided with the top of the door. It wasn't designed, I guess, for people of my height. I quickly recovered, or at least I acted so. Once I was in, I realized that I was going to stick with the girl for longer than a day or night, and in the end it turned out to be a whole six months.

She pointed me to a tiny armchair and walked up the stairs, which were twisted a little and lacked a handrail, so that if you stumbled on them, you might end up on the flowery tiled floor with broken bones. The narrow stairs had tiny flower vases on alternate steps, and one very small white dustbin was placed at the corner of the third step. I had never seen such a tiny one in my whole life, but that wasn't the only thing that was new to me with that girl. The home was as flowery in appearance and scent inside as it was outside. It was a very artistic home, I would say, but very full of stuff and very tiny, so that one couldn't take a few continuous steps without tripping over something. The light yellow wall was mostly covered with beautiful paintings of nature. Next to the main door hung a square box that said in colourful letters "Lord Bless This Mess". A delightful petite mini bar stood in the empty space under the stairs, with one gold-threaded decorated chair beside it. Adjacent to this was a small cabinet with glass doors that was stuffed with marble statues of people and animals. On top of the cabinet was a round silvery mirror wiped clean, and a big glass bowl in which two cat statues were placed. Close to the cabinet was the only armchair in the house, small and covered in light-red material. Opposite to this was a big-screen TV, and the space separating the two was mostly occupied by an oval-shaped glass table.

My nose was struck by a scent it had never perceived before. The girl was descending the stairs wearing a different dress, a short-sleeved, round-necked, knee-length thin grey cotton dress. I didn't give much thought to it at the time. She asked me to follow her and went out through a door-less opening to the back garden and kitchen. Again my forehead knocked against the top of the opening, and then I realized that the whole house was only suitable for dwarfs like her. The appropriate word when describing her home would be "small".

I stepped onto the cemented area of the secret backyard garden. She directed me to sit on a wooden chair.

"Litsea Cubeba," she said, while putting a steel bowl on the small stove.

"Pardon me?" I said. My eyes were jumping from one plant to another in the greenery of the garden. It was so magnificent and uplifting, as if a piece of imaginary paradise spot had appeared on earth. A white-brown cat started walking among the flowers and approached my feet with a yawning mouth. Surprisingly it had one green eye and one blue! Even the cat hadn't missed out on the artistic touches.

"My name is Litsea Cubeba." She was working on the cup of tea she had invited me for.

"Gerald." I shut my mouth to suppress the laughter that was about to emerge on hearing her name. *Litsea Cubeba!* I repeated in my mind.

"Litsea Cubeba?" Now it came out my mouth. Does any such name exist? Are we allowed to name our children any shit that crosses our mind? I had always thought that Russian names were the most difficult to pronounce.

"Hey, it is true! Litsea Cubeba. Strange name, isn't it? But a unique one."

The noise of the spoon colliding with the glass announced the readiness of my tea. She turned around and put two cups of tea on the tiny round table that barely had space for both cups. She sat opposite with one leg crossed atop the other. The shiny whiteness of her upper leg was attractively pure and apparently smooth. My eyes rested upon her dress in the particular area of her chest. It presented in a charismatic manner the perfect roundness and exact shape of the two young breasts and the perfect curves of her cleavage area. Her thin dress made it impossible to imagine a single wire of bra underneath and suggested she had none. But how proudly her breasts stood without any support! So superb.

"So you are a balloon maker?" She reached back and picked a red rose from the garden.

In that position the shadow of her flat nipple emerged, and I felt my lust growing even more. She adjusted herself back and started gently rubbing the rose with her thumb. The rounded shapes of the petals were highly suggestive of Litsea Cubeba's full-bloomed mature body, the redness provoked thoughts in me of her tiny lips in my mouth, and the opening and closing of the petals under the influence of her fingers evoked the dreamy image of the opening and closing of her vulva under my influence.

I nodded with a smile. "And you are a gardener?"

"Not really. I am a perfumer."

"A perfumer? Interesting," I commented.

She took her tea and sipped it, and remembering mine, I did the same, but that single sip didn't go in properly and so I had to spit it out.

"Is it tea?" I said, wiping my mouth with the bottom of my T-shirt.

"It is tea with myrrh," she answered. "I like it. You don't have to force yourself to drink it if you cannot."

I really wasn't going to take another sip from it, even if it meant not bedding her.

"My father used to be a good perfumer."

She started to tell her story while that unpleasant taste still lurked on my tongue. I forced myself to stop swallowing for the sake of giving her some respect and then built things upon that.

So, her father was a passionate Lebanese perfumer and one of the best in his time in the country. He went to Taiwan to start a perfumery business, and her mother was his secretary in a small company he established there. Working overtime together resulted in them developing feelings for each other, the fruit of which came in China during a work visit, when she found out that she was one month pregnant. Happiness captured the parents, marriage followed, and they both prayed for a girl. Being in China, the origin of the Litsea Cubeba plant, and the father's fondness for it, led to the decision to name his daughter after it. So it in the end it happened to be a girl and the name had already been decided upon since the first month of pregnancy. The mother was fond of lavender; lavender was everywhere in her life, and if she had the choice she would have named her child lavender.

Their marriage soon started to deteriorate, however, and one incident made the father open his eyes belatedly to his wife. That was when she tried to poison him, but he survived. This incident taught him to hate her, but he peacefully separated from his wife. The incident also halted his research and work as a perfumer, and he disregarded lavender specifically. The first time he came into contact with the hostile scent of lavender was when little Litsea Cubeba came home one day home holding a lavender flower. The father had an immediate heart attack, but once again he survived. His unfortunate reaction to the lovely scent of lavender happened once again when he was shopping for fruits in a supermarket that happened, for the first time in its history, to be selling lavender flowers. Another heart attack occurred, but this time it sent him to his grave. Litsea Cubeba inherited nothing from her father. All his fortune went to the mother under an old forgotten will that found her father giving his wife all rights to his entire fortune. Litsea Cubeba (and I find myself forced to use her full first name always for the sake of the plant it represents) built her life alone.

She finished her story and started sipping her tea.

"I learned perfumery on my own, you see."

"I see."

Time was passing, and I found that I hadn't got any closer to her. I had to break the dampness of the positively charged tranquillity in the air. I could read the sly shyness in her to finish what she had started when she asked me in. I believed she had in mind what I had, and I was thinking now of a way to break the ice so that rather than being strangers, we should become adventurers seeking zest of the flesh. But then the hoped-for initiative came, to my relief, from her. Her tiny foot caressed my knee and its fingers started pinching there.

"I always like to have a massage. It keeps me relaxed." A bright smile appeared on her round face. "Do you know how to massage, balloon man?"

"The hands that worked on balloons have experience working with so many things."

"Have they?"

She stood and walked inside, giving no signal for me to follow except for the shared thought in our minds of our hidden desire. I walked after her, and my forehead again hit the top of the opening. She walked up the scary stairs and so did I. She opened the door located just at the last step of the staircase, and I discovered that there was only one room on the second floor. A whiff of cosy citrusy scent struck my nose. The four walls of the room were painted in a different colour each, all of them light—green, pink, yellow, and violet—and on each coloured wall hung a framed dried flower the same colour as the wall—a green rose, a light-pink rose, a yellow rose, and a lavender rose.

"Lavender!" I said.

"Yes. It is still one of my favourites."

The room was quite spacious, and it was one more element of fantasy-like magic in that fairy home. A small pink painted book shelf stood along the pink wall, and I could read all the books' titles about perfumery. Colourful scented pillow sachets in small plates were placed on the dressing table and on small stands on each side of the bed. What was special about the bed was that the mattress, as I learned later, was stuffed with rose leaves and lavender flowers. What human wouldn't enjoy sleeping in such a bed?

Litsea Cubeba went to the bathroom and brought out a towel and a bottle of massage oil. I didn't believe till then that she really needed a massage. I thought it would be just direct sex, but nonetheless it was important, as the scene was becoming more fascinating and our time together more interesting. She pulled off her dress, and my eager gaze saw that she had no underwear. Pulling the light-red blanket aside, she lay on the bed on her tummy. Everything was scented in her house, and so was her body. Behind her left shoulder was a small tattoo of blue rose.

"Please me," she said in low voice, crossing her hands under her head.

I had never massaged anyone before, but I had watched a video about vulva massage in my time in college. I poured the scented oil on her back, and my inexperienced hands started rubbing for a couple of minutes. Her smooth skin became shiny and slippery, and my eyes couldn't stop staring at her small round buttocks, the left side of which bore a rash of tiny red pimples.

"Please me, Gerald." The tone was harder now.

I was already churning with lust. My oiled hands seized and squeezed those two buttocks and dug in between. I rolled her over and started stroking with oil her small flat-nippled melons. I slowly dragged one hand down her belly till my palm found its destination on her well-paved vulva. I stroked the outer and inner lips and more. My fingers put her on fire, and her moaning, shivering, and damp wetness caused erotic tension to rise within me and surely within her. Sliding my fingers in strained her body even more. Her head drifted backwards, her shoulders pushed up, her hand tightened around my elbow, and lovely beads of sweat covered her flushed crimson skin. The moments between her groans were quickly growing shorter, and they aroused an intense thirst in me, so that I forgot myself, jumped on my prey, and consumed all of her.

I opened my eyes in the evening and the fascinating image of Fang was in my mind. How strange it was that her image sensually reappeared in my mind from time to time. I turned my head, expecting to see Fang by me, but instead I saw Litsea Cubeba. Though I felt a slight hidden disappointment, I didn't regret sleeping with the new girl. I put my hand on her bare chest to reward myself for what I got for the day. I closed my eyes to fall back to sleep, but a second scene appeared in front of me that alarmed me; it was that deadly haunting image from the dreadful past of my father covered in my mother's blood. My eyes were now wide open, and an itching fear struck my heart of the kind that I had only experienced when thinking of that scene. I pulled my hand back off the chest, and the fast motion, I guess, disturbed Litsea Cubeba. She yawned and rubbed her eyes and checked the clock on the small table beside the bed.

"Eight." She yawned again, and tears appeared in her eyes. "You are already awake? Haven't you enjoyed your sleep with me?"

"I surely did. It was only a nightmare."

"A nightmare on such a day? How disappointing!"

She threw the blanket over me in a joking gesture and got out of the bed and went into the bathroom. Her short naked body glittered under the dim light of the room, and her tits jumped, as before, up and down. I smelled a little sweaty, but she of roses; I guess the rose petals in the mattress had their chemistry with her body. One tiny petal strangely, and I don't know from where, was glued in the area between her buttocks. I jumped out of the bed and removed that red paper from where it was lost and misplaced. That motion hurled her body forward and forced a scream out her mouth, which was followed by a loud giggle.

I walked to the other end of the room, where the only window was covered with a floral curtain. I withdrew it a little and caught sight of an image from the next home of a family—mother, father, and young son—sitting at a table, eating and sharing laughter. It stirred a wave of sadness within me for not being able to recall when was the last time in my childhood I had similar joy with my parents. I blessed the family in my heart and wished the son a pure life, unlike mine. I let the curtain fall back and turned to a slim closet on the floor nearby. I sat down and opened its tiny door with two fingers, and then I had one more surprise about Litsea Cubeba. It contained some DVDs of massage porn. Now I could see where she was coming from when she asked me to massage her.

At that point Litsea Cubeba came out the shower room with the purple floral towel in her hands, rubbing her hair dry. She wasn't wearing any garment yet. A few dew drops were flowing onto the glassy surface of her golden body. She was holding a bottle of oil.

"Would you like to massage my breasts?" she asked, shaking the bottle.

I stared at her for a while, and she stared back at me, and our eyes examined each other's naked bodies. We both smiled at the same moment. I nodded, and she approached and sat on the edge of the bed and handed me the oil bottle. I climbed onto the bed and rested on my knees, which were attached behind her. My penis started hardening against her back, and I realized that she could feel it, but it was all part of a process she desired, I guess.

"What is this?" I asked, looking at the oil's green hue.

"This is grape seed oil mixed with sweet almond. Added to that are some herbal oils. This blend is my creation and invention. It helps maintain the shape, size, and firmness of the breasts."

I could now see the secret behind her perfectly shaped breasts. I opened the bottle and poured some oil in my palms and started in a random way to massage her breasts. After a while they started to slip through my palms like balls of jelly. My hand could sense the symphony of her heartbeat playing in stronger pulses as the process continued, and I saw that even my inexperienced hands had some magical effect.

"We should always anoint our chest because it is the realm of the heart." Her tone strived to stay normal, but it showed extreme softness.

The breast-massaging session was over, and she asked me to lie down on the bed. She pulled out some expensive civet oil and brushed it on my genitals, which made me wonder whether she was feeling the sexual desire I had for the second sex of the evening or whether it was just the mere idea of sharing crazy massages. That civet smelled very bad to my taste, but shockingly she followed with deep licking and sucking. She reminded me of Bram Stoker's blood-sucking Dracula character. Who would like licking an animal? She did!

The next day, she asked me to work with her and I instantly agreed, having an interest in learning something about the field of scent and perfumery. She had a room downstairs on the ground floor, hidden by a door half the height of any other dwarf-size door in the house. Once I stepped inside, one single word was always the king of the realm—scent. I had heard that there was a whole new world to discover in the making of perfume, and I saw how much truth was in that saying. In her laboratory everything had a name, and its meaning derived from the special characteristic that its scent has provided. So many bottles were located on different shelves. She had the raw undiluted essential oils, along with her finished products. She told me that the bulb-type bottles were her alcohol-based perfumes, while the dark glasses held her oil-based perfumes. Her creativity didn't stop in making perfumes; she made modified products for body lotions, shampoos, massage oils, hair treatment oils, and other purposes. There I discovered the captivating powers of essential oils; the powers that rendered joy and mirth and fill our senses to the brim.

I started my learning process making perfume. Litsea Cubeba explained to me that any perfume has three notes—the top, the heart, and the base. The top note is weak and gives the first impression of the perfume; the heart note adds body to a blend; and the base note is used to add lifespan to a blend. Litsea Cubeba had her essential oils properly categorized on her shelves. The top notes were wrapped with yellow paper tape, the middle notes with blue, and the base notes with red.

She had loyal customers who would visit her and buy some selected products, or they would tell her about the occasion for which they wanted the perfume, and Litsea Cubeba would apply her experience, knowledge, and creativity in creating the right blend. Litsea Cubeba would order her essential oils from different suppliers, and when I asked her about it, she said that different suppliers have different qualities of certain essential oils. Not all suppliers sell the same quality of a certain oil. As the price of essential oils was fairly high, so were the perfumes and different blends that she made. Litsea Cubeba was making enough money and more from her trade, and I was getting paid not only for sharing my working hands, but also for sharing her bed.

It seemed that every blend she made fit her skin, especially those floral ones. When her skin interacted with the base notes of these, it brought out a comforting odour. Living and working with her for six months had its effect on me as well; she had a new effect upon me, and essential oils surrounded me and engulfed every aspect of my daily life. If I was seen with some insect bites, she would bring me eucalyptus oil. When she saw me privately thinking, she would bring me grapefruit or bergamot or rose absolute, saying that they were solutions for my depression. For my headache she would offer rosemary oil, and the same rosemary would be mixed in massage oil for my muscle stiffness. Some nights she would bring me clary sage, saying that it would help me sleep.

"People with anosmia tend to get depressed more often because of lack of essence in their world," she told me once.

Daily at home different smells would produce the atmosphere; juniper, eucalyptus, and sandalwood are a few I could mention. I recall once I applied orange oil to a spot on my shoulder just prior to going to the beach on a sunny day. That spot burned like hell, to the amusement of Litsea Cubeba, who advised me later to avoid direct contact with sunlight after applying undiluted essential citrus oils on the skin. It took me almost a month to fully recover from the darkened effect of that burn.

One day when we were in a mall, she complained that the smell there was disturbing for her nerves, although the smell in the air was only of some sort of corn. She took a small dark bottle from her purse and started inhaling from it. Disregarding my advice to avoid doing that in public, she continued to do it from time to time until a police officer approached us, and we were taken to a police station on suspicion of using illegal drugs. It took her two hours to explain to the police the good nature of her deed in order for us to be let out free. She thanked me for my earlier advice once we walked out, but I guess she didn't learn from that mistake. One day she started ordering large quantities of essential oils online, and again she ignored my suggestion not to do so, only to find out that she was called in by the police after one week and questioned about the intended use of the large quantities ordered. She was suspected this time of some planned terrorist act. Poor girl!

I was myself transformed into a walking open bottle of perfume. I smelled sweeter than usual, but I had lost my old personal essence. Litsea Cubeba would recognize me approaching her, not by hearing my footsteps, but by recognizing the scent she anointed me with. I became more like a pet, I guess, or one of her essential oil bottles that she could recognize with her eyes closed by a single sniff. I hated that and decided to follow the thread of my depression and leave that girl who was so full of scents but had no scent of herself.

I wouldn't miss anything about Litsea Cubeba. I had gained a few skills about perfumery, and one memory burned me with craving for two months after leaving her—the memory of the early mornings when she would sit in her garden and sip that myrrh tea, wearing a knee-length skirt flushed with darker and lighter plain pink roses over a shadowy black background. On top she would wear a light pink sleeveless blouse with the chest open wide enough to vividly unveil the lovely white skin, with the top line of her cleavage clearly visible. What enticed me more was the way the blouse fell over her fine mid-sized bra-less breasts, demonstrating the god-sent beauty of a woman's breasts. That tickling cosy curve was so captivating, and it was as much arousing for me to see it veiled as it would have been unveiled. She never liked to wear bras at home; her reason was that they hindered her breathing. Oh, it might for her, but for me it was a source of pleasure to stare at her chest stealthily, even knowing that I would bed her in the end over and over.

24

$\mathcal{I}$ went back to China, bearing in mind the two years of my life that remained. I didn't know where I would get stuck next in my journey to find things of interest, and I preferred to stick to the country where I planned to have the last stop of my life illustrated. I started writing a book, *The Way to Suicide*, which consists of a collection of essays about the uselessness of life and living and the light that death opens in the eyes of those who select the path of suicide. I didn't know and I don't know yet whether somebody would eventually agree to publish it. The same is true of this biographical book that my pen disobeys me in writing. However, I believe that it is all about freedom of belief and expression when it comes to literature. We should be able to speak our hearts and write about the things that eat us up, the things that provide us ecstasy, and the things that implant in us thorns of agony. For me it has always been the agony of death and dying that has drugged my pen. I could have chosen to research and write about painting, guitar, writing, programming, perfumery, or any other subject, but nothing ever affected me as deeply as the art of dying.

Weakened by a strange hazy feeling of overcoming my hatred, I attended to a call of duty and went to the graveyard where my parents are buried. How beautiful is its spacious green landscape, and the earthy aroma is more captivating than the breezes of beaches. The scattered white rectangles of different sizes add artistic comeliness. How exquisite are the plants of the graveyard and how abundantly the greenery spreads there! I guess the soil of the graveyard is not dead like the corpses underneath, or perhaps it is the dead that provide that vigorous fertility to the normally insignificant soil of earth.

It took me almost thirty minutes to locate them. The graves of my terrible parents lay flatter to the ground more than most of those around them, and they were heavily covered with husks and dust. I stood there at their feet and in a split second felt I had fulfilled their hungry request to come there. I don't believe in God and an afterlife, but still I believe that their spirits would suffer under the heavy layers of earth, and I wouldn't regret a bit seeing them suffer for the evil of their characters. My eyes located the empty space to the right of my mother's grave, and a strange desire stroke me for my body to be buried there after my death. I hated the thought and idea of it.

To stir up my dead feelings even more bitterly, I went to the company my father used to work for, a small private software-development company. I provided my CV, which I had updated on the plane to China. It was eleven in the morning when I reached the glass door of the building. A young lady was standing just beside it with a portion of her body covering the push bar, elegantly dressed with appropriately applied makeup, except for a dark pink highlight on the eyebrows. She stared at me and smiled, and I looked at the briefcase in her hand. My initial thought was that she was also seeking a job. I didn't pay much attention to her. I reached behind her and pushed the bar, forcing the door open. As soon as the opening was wide enough for a normal human body to fit through, the lady slid in without even saying a word of excuse or thanks. It was as if she was waiting for me or somebody else to open the door for her, she being a princess I guess. Once inside, she walked away quickly, and my eyes caught sight of her shaking bottom.

I walked in and took the stairs, and my eyes just roamed around, trying to recall how the place had looked when first my father took me with him to his workplace. I was very young back then, but still a portion of that memory came to me. My father liked to use stairs always for their health benefits. I recalled him holding my small hand and walking slowly up the staircase. I reached the third floor, the floor that his company occupied, and the small curved reception desk was facing me. My father's voice came into my mind, introducing me to the young lady there, and I could see the same lady still there with the same thin body but with deeper age lines. I smiled and greeted her, and she returned my greeting the same way she had done before. I asked her where I could turn in my résumé, and as she reached for it, a female voice called her, asking her for all the résumés available. The receptionist turned, and so did I, to see the lady I had met down outside the building. She looked at me and then at the résumé in my hand that I was about to pass to the receptionist.

"May I look at it?" the lady asked.

I could see she was not just a normal employee. I handed her my papers, and the receptionist handed her all other résumés she had in her drawer.

"You can follow me," the lady said and started to walk back.

I followed her along the corridor through the office cubes. Some passing employees greeted her with respect. She entered a big glass office and asked me to sit.

"I am Hua Xu. I'm the manager here."

She set aside all the other résumés she was holding and put mine in front of her on the desk. I didn't say anything. My name was already on the paper and I found it silly to mention it. She went through my papers and kept throwing sharp glances at me as she did so.

"Writer, programmer, guitar player . . . and . . . ha!" She paused and busied herself again with her eyes buried in my papers. "What are you, Gerald Thin?"

Well, Gerald Thin was the name I had used on my résumé. I just wished to hide my family name.

"I am anything that fits a post, and I can be anything. For a post in this company, I am a programmer."

"A programmer!" Hua said, and then she remained silent for a few seconds while staring at me. "I'm not sure how a creative person like you can fit into such a small company that doesn't fulfil your ambitions, but I can see you will be needed here. One post only is available for now, and you have it."

"Thank you," I calmly said without any single indication of appreciation.

"Your work starts tomorrow."

She took the rest of the résumés and placed them in the box allocated for recycling paper. How quickly I had got what I had so little hope for! A small part of me was happy for what I saw as a sign of being ridiculously sick in my mind for coming there in the first place. I went out the glass-walled room and walked among the office cubes. An image my eyes had captured years ago appeared in my mind of me holding the finger of my father and walking there with him, making jokes here and there with other employees. My feet stopped at a picture with not-so-good quality. A large group of employees was standing in a green field with a big poster at their back showing the name of the company, "Blooming". I narrowed my eyes and gazed at the faces. My father was among them. I withdrew instantly and took my eyes off it.

"Ho ho ho," a voice came from behind me, and a hand was placed on the back of my shoulder.

I turned to see a man in his early fifties, roughly dressed with narrow eyes, most of which was covered with bushy white eyebrows. He wore thin glasses and had a thin smiling mouth.

"Careful, son."

"Sorry." I said, and I started to walk away when he spoke again.

"Do I know you, young boy?"

I paused and looked at his face. It wasn't a bit familiar to me. I shook my head and resumed my steps.

When I reached my apartment, I got a call on my cell phone. I answered it. It was Hua. She asked me to come to Blooming the next day by seven in the morning, saying that she would brief me about a few rules of the company. I did reach the company at seven the next day, and strangely no other employee was around on the single floor the company occupied, not even the receptionist. I went to Hua's glass office, but it was empty as well. I thought that she might have felt too lazy to wake up early as the office hours didn't start until eight-thirty. I was about to leave when I heard her voice.

"Good morning," she said.

She was holding a cup of coffee. With a half-smile she went into her office and placed the cup slowly on one side of her well-organized desk. She talked to me, but not about any rules of the company. To my surprise she just talked rubbish—nothing related to work, but everything related to me. Many of her irritating personal questions I answered with complete lies. I could see what she was aiming at—to please herself with me. I wouldn't have any objection to that. I would enjoy having a casual affair with a hot workmate, but I hated the cheapness of her approach in hiring an employee for the sake of lying between his legs.

As time passed, a number of employees started to arrive, and the middle-aged man who had spoken to me the day before was there as well. He smiled at me, shook hands with me, and greeted me heartily. I returned his greetings, but I had no wish to talk to him in any mysterious fashion, the way he had on my last visit.

"I had some time yesterday night. My wife had been busy the whole day correcting a heap of exam papers," he said. "I thought about you and where I had seen you. My mind isn't as strong as it used to be, you see. I know your face because it reminds me of an old friend of mine, Leo Arsov."

It struck me hard to hear him say my father's name. Under normal circumstances, having a job in a company my father worked in, this would not have been a surprise, but his recognising any resemblance between me and my father was very upsetting. Millions of times have I seen myself in mirror, but I could never see any similarity between us. I couldn't see how that guy could see any. Is it that when we deny who we really are that we forget who we are? Or it is the truth of us that pure-hearted people see? I wanted to be nothing like my father. I even believed I was one step higher than him in morality, though I don't trust much in moralities.

"What's your name, son?" he asked.

"Gerald," I almost whispered.

"Oh, Gerald Arsov. What a name! Are you the one Leo brought in as child? Yes, I guess you are. Who else would have the same good looks as you? Oh God, my memory gets worse by the day. The memories of your father are escaping my mind. So do all the memories of all the good things I've experienced in life." He scratched his white-haired head and then reached out his hand again. "I am Jian."

I shook hands with him again, but I wanted to get away from him, and so I excused myself, giving no more details about myself and him asking for no more. But I felt a liking for Jian because of the pure and kind character he demonstrated. Walking around between the office cubes, I was struck to find that most of the employees there were middle-aged or old-aged. It seemed as if my father alone was missing among his work colleagues. It didn't matter much that I was working with older people once they accepted me and considered me part of the family. They would call me "son", which happily replaced my real name which most of the employees there didn't know any more, and Jian, that quietly smiling character, didn't speak of my identity to anyone there, as if reading my mind. The current manager, Hua Xu, was the daughter of the deceased earlier manager, whom, unlike others in the company, age didn't forgive.

Hua—yes, it is true, reader—became my bed comrade on a weekend basis. Who could ask for more than that from his manager! And as she wished to demonstrate herself as the manager in the office, she did the same in bed. But never mind that! Pleasure was my ultimate aim with her, nothing more.

After one month of working at Blooming, I could see how badly the company was managed. The aged employees were incapable of keeping up with market demand; the production capability was weak, and the reason was the age of the employees, who would share empathies and cosy chats with each other instead of sharing and talking about actual work. They were getting their salaries cheap, and they were glad of it. Where else could they spend time with friends and get paid for it?

Once, after bedtime with Hua, I raised the subject of the company's productivity. What else could she do, she asked. All the employees there were close friends of her deceased father, and they had been very kind with her when she was young. Her heart insisted that she be kind to them. What an answer from an educated manager! If all managers were as emotional as her, I guess the business of the country would be sent to the gallows.

For six months I lived among those half-dead employees. My work varied from nothing to just little insignificant tasks. I would come to the office and bring books with me; reading was more interesting to me than listening to the old radios throw out their repetitious subjects. Ultimately, being passive bored me, and so I took a new step to add some value to my work. I started developing games for mobile phones, and once a few were ready for use, I went marketing them on the Internet under the company name in the best interests of the company, without any mention of my own name. Well it went well, and the fruits of my efforts started blooming in Blooming. I brought the company customers, young with ideas and expectations, within two months of starting to market the games. It took a hell of effort from me, but it was worth it. Hua Xu was very proud of the achievement and celebrated the event, and my aged colleagues were very happy to see their "son" with such an accomplishment. They were all so glad for what I had done, but I wasn't.

"Leo Arsov," one of them said in the celebration, remembering my father, I guess.

"Yes," another answered.

I looked at Jian among the crowd, and he nodded, but after the celebration he told me that my father had been the best among them all, and like me, he had brought a new change to the company. But the thing was that apart from him, none of those employees noticed the similarity of physical complexion between me and my father. Age played a big role, I guess.

I discussed with Hua that night in bed the idea of recruiting some new young ambitious employees in place of some of her current employees. She agreed on the first point but discarded the second. Well, she was the decision-maker in the end, and managers normally don't like to be told to make a certain decision.

But as I expected, it turned ugly. The company spent money recruiting three young employees, who just happened to have finished college a month ago and who happened to be distant relatives of Hua. There was a big similarity between the new employees and those aged ones; both parties showed minimal interest in work. My efforts to raise the name of Blooming were in vain. It seemed that it was impossible to fix anything in that aging ailing company. I made up my mind and left the company after one full year of wasted time working there.

25

$\mathcal{T}$he sky was dropping scattered but large drops of rain. When one drop touched the sensitive skin of your face, you would really feel its vigour and weight. The wind from the east was gentle, too weak to disturb the rain drops but it felt lovely and welcome when it brushed the skin. The fragrance of the air was slightly disturbed by the smell of soil that covered the sides of the pavement, but it did nothing to affect the pleasant feeling that the overall atmosphere had bestowed upon me. My hair felt freshened and skin enlightened as I walked down the pavement wearing shorts and a T-shirt. I had a smile set deeply on my face. Nature sometimes overwhelms us with its simple beauties that no disastrous plan can withhold.

I had in front of me a lifespan of one year—one more year to get the shit of me out of the dirt of life. But that wouldn't sadden me a bit or move me an inch. We all walk to our destinies, and my destiny had been fixed during the days of my childhood.

I was walking that day to a flower shop near my apartment to liven up my dull brown painted room. Yellow and red roses would fit the brown background well in my imagination.

When I entered the flower shop, a figure caught my eye—a female body whose complexion was not so strange to me but was stored among the heap of memory files in my mind. Her white blouse was tucked in a long tight pink skirt. Though it was elegant enough to my eyes and taste, my mind seemed to fail me in putting together the pieces as I reflected about who that girl resembled. I wasn't looking for any new hot figure to disturb the inner peace of my heart, so I just started carefully picking my flowers. At that moment while I was waiting for my flowers to be wrapped, the girl's voice, paying at the cashier's desk a few steps from me, caught my ears, and instantly the fine figure of a girl rose to the top of my memory.

"You should give me a discount this time," she argued loudly. "I am always coming here. I'm a regular customer and buying more from you than most customers, and yet I don't get a decent discount . . ."

"Miss . . ." the young girl at the counter tried to interrupt her, when she herself got interrupted.

"Li Chou," I whispered to myself, recalling her name.

"My friend came here yesterday, and she said that she got a good discount. Why not me? Why are you against me?"

"Li Chou." I called her name as I walked to her. She turned and smiled broadly as she looked at me.

"Who is this guy?" she clasped her hands, before spreading them before her and walking quickly towards me.

We hugged swiftly and then pulled away to face each other.

"You are back," she whispered, and her hands loosely gripped my fingers, which I gladly allowed.

"I am."

"Where do you live?" She asked, and her shy smile covered her face.

"Nearby. Where do you work?"

"For a while I worked at Blooming, as the manager there is a family friend. That company is very small in space and in results. Now I work as a network administrator in a European-owned private company, but I often think of leaving it and seeking a different path in life."

We paused for a while and stared at each other.

"I see you are having a good discussion with the girl." I nodded towards the girl at the counter.

"Oh, no. You heard that? Nothing here protects the consumer's rights."

I now placed my wrapped flowers on the cashier's desk. I looked at the girl with a tender smile.

"Will you please give us a discount?" I said with the charm required for the moment.

"Okay, sir," said the ugly counter girl.

Li approached and was about to open her mouth to start a new argument, I guess, when I placed my hand on her back and pressed it there. She took it, as I intended, as an indication to keep quiet, and she closed her lips. We went out and stood under the thin shade the shop provided. She looked down and picked a yellow umbrella at the side of the door.

"Is it yours?" I asked, doubting for a while any answer that would agree.

"Hmm," Li answered. "I just forgot it here."

She leaned a little forward as she opened the umbrella, and the figure of this girl who was once a student of mine lit a spark that energized and awoke all my senses with a shock of current. I could see how her white blouse and pink skirt still fitted her and gave her fine figure a pleasant appearance. I could see that I might not be able to keep myself from caressing tits and cunts for the rest of my life journey as I had promised myself.

Li was as tidy in her dress and speech as she had been when a student. Nothing had changed in her during my absence. Her straight hair was still the same length, her lips carried the same natural redness, the same blush brushed her cheeks, and the shape of her body hadn't changed a bit. Even her not fully mature character remained the same, but that always suited my taste. I had never been attracted to a girl with roughness or a manly strength of character. It is the special softness of femininity that is in the best of taste. But wait! There was one thing that had changed in her character: she was shyer. She used to be more daring and expose her character as a student, but she was very quiet now. Or was it that she was shy now that she was with me without the boundaries of teacher and student?

During the minute we walked side by side under the yellow umbrella, I kept wondering how far I might go with Li and whether it was right to feed myself upon her at this stage of my life, even though at that moment I could swear that she, even if just for a split second, had a wicked fantasy of having sex with me. It was undeniable. Her dead silence all of a sudden and her heavier blushing made it clear that something of that sort was tickling her lust and breeding in her mind. The drops of rain hammered in slow motion on the top of our narrow roof, and I thought for a couple of seconds that they would tear their way through it.

"Would you like to eat something?" I asked.

"Actually I am going to my grandmother's. She asked me to bring her flowers. Would you like to come with me?"

"Where?"

"To my grandma's. She is a peaceful old lady, and she will be happy to see you with me."

The question "why" lingered in my mind, but I didn't wish to say it. We walked in silence again. One side of my arm was touching hers, and my partially wet hair was dripping at the back of my neck, forming a path that tickled along the line of my back.

We reached a decent red house, and the doorbell was answered by an old lady whose aged face and the slightly bent back concealed the strength of her body. The grandmother kissed Li and shook hands with me.

"Hi, handsome," she said, and as I felt the force of her hand, she looked in my eyes and smiled, as if showing off her ageless power.

I followed Li into the house and to a sofa. Turning around, I expected to see the grandma following slowly behind us, but I had an amazing shock when my eyes caught her small figure moving quickly towards the kitchen. Since when could turtles run? I couldn't believe it, and when I looked at Li, she smiled and leaned her head to one side.

"She is a superwoman, you see." Li said and placed her lower lip under the top one while wearing the same smile.

The running turtle appeared from the kitchen holding a tray with two glasses of juice. She placed it on the table and sat opposite us on a rocking chair with a long back rest. The old lady looked like the skeleton of a princess left over for decades who had once been on a throne.

"You seem to have found a man at last," the old lady said and leaned to pick up her glasses and a thick bible-like book.

"He was my teacher, Gerald Arsov," Li commented quickly to forestall any allegation from her grandma that I was her boyfriend.

The grandmother, having heard my name, gave me with a hard look. The smile on her face faded for a while, and her mouth opened. She felt frightened somehow, but then she recollected herself and her simple smile returned.

"Your teacher," she said and then released a quick cough.

"He was my . . ." Li started loudly, but then the volume of her voice went down. "Favourite teacher."

"You stay here, daughter," the grandma said, looking at Li, and she stood up from her chair. "Your father will be visiting in a couple of hours. I have to go to my yoga class."

"But today is Friday; you don't have classes on Friday," said Li.

"I have today. Give some clothes to Gerald so he can change. He may catch cold in his wet dress. Have a good day, young man." She quickly walked out of the house.

"I am very sorry, Gerald. How did I miss seeing your wet clothes? Come, you may borrow some of my father's."

I walked behind her to one of the rooms. Li opened a closet. "I don't know what's wrong with her. Suddenly she gets upset for no reason."

"She is an old lady after all."

"I guess so." She took out a pair of shorts and a T-shirt. "You can borrow these."

"What for? It is better I leave now," I said.

"Why?" The question came loud, but she lowered her voice once more as she continued. "You will not be having lunch with us?"

"Well, if only I am invited."

"You are," she responded instantly. "Haven't I mentioned that?" She reached out to hand me the clothes.

"I guess you didn't."

I didn't know exactly whether she was just assuming that I could always read her thoughts and that I would do what I was expected to in her mind, or if it was just acting at the right moment. But I was even more certain that she wished to be with me. I wished the same because of the deep respect I naturally carried for her. She was a really decent girl, but the strength of the taboos raised by my respect for her didn't stop me having a secret lust for licking her warm flesh.

"So you are staying?" Her mouth remained open at the end of the half question.

"I am."

I took the clothes from her hands and nodded to her. She giggled happily in a semi-muted tone and drew the door half-closed as she went out. I took off my wet spotted grey shorts and then my blue T-shirt and rubbed my hair dry with the latter, before piling them on the floor that felt cold under my bare feet. Unzipping the white shorts she had provided, I slid my legs into them, I zipped them up round my waist; they fitted me almost perfectly. I pushed my head through the neck opening of the T-shirt, and as I pulled my hands through, my eyes suddenly caught sight of a picture on the wall of a normal-looking guy with a thick moustache and hands resting backwards on the front of a green Hummer vehicle. A vague fierce current of hard feeling went through me, accompanied by a flow of inner heat through my throat. Feeling dizzy and as if I was about to throw up, I quickly located the bed and collapsed on it, producing a loud bang as I fell on it, the bed being very low to the floor. I stopped myself from falling back and covered my eyes with my palms. Suddenly, with hidden horrors, images of blood appeared in front of me, and their taste ran in my mouth. I forced open my eyes and the sound of the door opening rang in my ears. I thought at first it was the effect of the turbulent emotional situation I was in, but then the figure of Fang stood in front of me for a second and then drew closer to me.

"What's wrong, Gerald? What's wrong?"

Two light hands were placed on my shoulders and I lifted my face to see Fang's bright face. Unconsciously, I dropped my hands around her waist and pressed my face against her flat belly. Tears ran from my eyes in irrational fear, as it seemed at the time. It was the first time, I guess, that I showed my tears to any of the girls I had been with, but it, wasn't the last.

"Fang . . ." came out my mouth.

"What happened?" she asked, slipping her fingers through my hair.

I then realized suddenly the world I was in, and opening my eyes on reality, the light-pink skirt reminded me of the identity of the girl I was holding. No Fang was near; there was only Li. I withdrew from her quickly and started wiping my eyes with the bottom of the T-shirt I had on.

She sat next to me. Her gentle fingers kept caressing my hair and my scalp.

"I will be with you no matter what is happening in your mind," Li said.

She pressed her face closer to mine, but her lips were visibly trembling. She didn't have the same courage now as she had when she was a student to kiss me, even on the cheek. Our eyes met for a while, and mine dropped to her lips; her top lip wiped the bottom, leaving it wet. I strongly felt she was my salvation from the current storm of hardness that had emerged. With force, I took those shy lips into mine, swallowed them, and licked hard the jewelled candy that presumably, for that short moment, belonged to me. But the glorious moment came when my action was met with a similar reaction. Li pressed her chest tight against mine so that her small breasts flattened and disappeared against my chest, and her heart bumped and bumped through her chest with a loud sound to my ears. The sweet fear that was capturing her about the deed she was involved in with a previous teacher caused her saliva drip into my mouth. This scene may seem disgusting and unnatural to some, but it is so sweet when it involves a man and a sweet angelic creature. I swallowed her dry mouth, and when I held her by her shoulders and detached myself from her, I could see how sweetly swollen her lips were, and her heavy breathing was enticing as if she had just completed some physical exercise. Her light brown eyes dropped to my lips as well, and she childishly chuckled.

There was no way, I guess, either of us could back off now. We had given ourselves to the demon of true lust when first our lips met—or, no, it was when I first accepted her invitation to accompany her to her grandmother's home. I truly didn't wish to take advantage of Li in any unethical manner, because she was a special gift looked at by my heart in the whole of my venture. She was like the sweetest dessert that one would keep for the end to savour most above all, and fate had reserved her for me at the end of my life. I drew my hand down her shoulder and paused at the top mound of her left breast. Her pure heart vibrated under my hand, and my latest motion produced a fascinating reaction from her. She lifted my T-shirt and hid her small head underneath, and her dry mouth created a cosy wet feeling as she sucked my breast and nipple like a child deprived for long from what it legitimately deserved. My one hand eagerly went to her back and removed the bra from her chest, while the other hand crawled down across her belly. Only then could I feel her firmly shaped abs; I never knew her to be a sports girl, but abs shaped this way on a girl always won my dislike and disapproval. The thought of caressing her belly withdrew from my mind, and I slid my hand lower, stretching the top elastic band of the panties and dropping those hungry fingers in.

Our clothes started flying off as the next step, and that young flower never ceased to tremble in my arms throughout the execution of the needed task, but all those trembles and the tears of pain she shed the whole time sweetened the whole process, because I realized she really enjoyed it despite her limited experience.

At the end of it all, she lay next to me. Both of us were open-eyed, but she gazed at the ceiling. I turned myself on one side and drew with the tip of my finger an imaginary line on the side of her neck.

"I have had casual sex a few times before when I got desperately and depressingly drunk, but nothing serious. My grandma always laughs at me, saying that I am not lucky in my love life," Li said.

I knew that she wasn't lucky with me either. She was the first girl for whom I had carried feelings both before and after intercourse. I couldn't see how to tell her that I really liked her, but it wouldn't be useful at all to admit it to her, seeing that I had just less than a year to live. Should I marry her, I wondered, and give her pain for the coming nine months. It would have surely brought me happiness, but it would have been very bad of me to do so and spoil her beautiful young life. I would have been selfish to make that decision, and that wasn't among the principles I believed in.

"Having this pure heart of yours, you surely will be lucky with your love life," I said.

"How do you know?" She turned her face now to face me.

"I can just see it."

A moment of fine silence followed while my nose enjoyed sniffing her damp skin that still bore some trace of a wonderful light perfume. Then I recalled the strange feeling I had experienced minutes before. I turned my face towards the picture hanging on the wall. Again a strange shock, though lighter, held me. I couldn't make out what that feeling was and the source of it. I did get strange feelings towards things around me from time to time, but never one so violent.

"Who is this moustached man?" I asked, my eyes still fixed on the picture.

"Oh," Li chuckled. "He is my father, Gen." Then after a pause she continued. "He is not much liked in our family, even though he is rich and clever. My grandmother doesn't favour him much because of his attitude towards the family. He is always drunk, and he is the kind of person who speaks his thoughts no matter how offensive they might be."

I giggled slowly. "So how does your mother stay with him?"

"I don't know my mother, to be honest. I was the product of him having casual sex with a strange woman, who ran away one month after giving birth to me because of the cruel treatment of my father. I really wish she had taken me with her, because the father I know I only meet once a month. Today is one of the exceptional days when I see my father in an unplanned way."

I wrapped my hand around her and placed a deep kiss on her lips. Her response was to lift her head a little off the pillow and return my kiss with a deep breath. Our new session of sharing lips was interrupted by the sound of the door alarm. In a fearful manner, Li pushed me and the nail of her thumb scratched through the skin on the top of my chest. She jumped out of the bed with the blanket wrapped around her, and her hands held it so as not to display any sign of her breasts and other critical areas, as if it wasn't me who had just nailed her minutes ago. She picked up all the scattered pieces of her clothes and ran into the bathroom.

"You put on your dress," she shouted. "Father is here."

I calmly followed her order. I didn't care about her father and grandmother for having sex with a fully grown-up girl. After all, having a casual sex is a decision made by two parties. I enjoyed watching her nervous actions.

She came out of the bathroom and started to comb her hair while at the same time adjusting her clothes.

"I will help you," I said as I took the comb from her hand and started running it through her shiny hair. Her arbitrary movements made it very difficult, and she exclaimed quietly in pain as the points of the comb came in contact with her scalp.

"Li . . ." the voice of the grandmother came from hall.

Li stood at the door of the room and beckoned me to follow her. We went out together and the fast-walking turtle was coming into the kitchen with a plastic bag in her hand. Li ran into the kitchen after her, leaving me behind, and started helping the old lady with the stuff in the bag. She was fascinating, that Li girl, and she deserved the best of life.

I walked to the sofas and switched on the unique yellow television. The news was on, and it was talking about a murder case, the victim of which was a young school girl. I listened to the Chinese commentator, whose nose seemed to be blocked as her voice sounded as if it was coming from deep in her throat. The young school girl was chopped into pieces and each piece was thrown in a different garbage bin across the city. It was horrible even to hear about it.

"This country is all about murders and murderers."

I turned to see the source of that comment and saw that a well-built, thick-moustached man was standing beside me with the palms of his hands spread. I stood on my feet, just as a sign of imaginary respect, and shook hands with him. He was the guy from the picture in the other room. He looked rougher than the picture, and his moustache had turned grey. His hand squeezed mine, and a sudden shock ran across my brain causing direct agony; once again the image of my father holding the heart of my mother had appeared. I quickly withdrew my hand from that big fist and dropped onto the sofa.

"Are you all right?" Gen asked and placed his hand on my shoulder.

"Yes," I nodded. "Just migraine." That was a lie.

Gen called his daughter to bring me a glass of water.

"He has had this headache since this morning," Li said, handing me a glass of water and sitting next to me. Her presence had a kind of soothing effect. "So, you have migraine and you didn't tell me about it!" she said, as if she was my girlfriend. But oh, I did wish to be her boyfriend, and I really did like the care that comment demonstrated for me.

Gen went to change his clothes, and the grandmother went into the kitchen to prepare lunch. I planted a quick kiss on Li's mouth, and she looked at me with a little frown. It was as if she knew everything about me, and the story of migraine was the missing piece in the whole puzzle picture.

"I don't have migraine. I just lied. I didn't feel good when I looked at your father. That's all."

She put her hand on her mouth and giggled.

"Who would feel good looking at my father?" she commented.

We gathered within minutes at a table for lunch. Li sat next to me, while on the opposite side were Gen and the grandmother.

"How is your head now?" Gen asked.

"The pain is over." I replied.

"I heard you are a teacher."

"I was."

"All my life I have hated teachers. No offence meant to you, but that is my true opinion. Teachers keep you away from truth and reality and fill your head with bullshit rubbish."

Li stopped eating and stared at her father angrily. I nudged her foot with mine, and she saw a smile on my face. Her father was certainly very opinionated, as the daughter had warned me.

"That might be the reason why I quit the job," I sarcastically commented.

Gen giggled and so did I, and Li's smile returned. But one thing didn't change—the hard look on the grandmother's face as if I wasn't welcome at the table and my presence was a heavy burden. I didn't mind that old witch. I liked Li and planned to stay close to her for some time before my death.

The thick-moustached guy delivered another of his opinions. He described the poor people roaming in the shopping malls with their simple or ragged dresses.

"They shouldn't be allowed to enter malls, I believe." He spoke while chewing a piece of chicken skin. "The malls should have a dress code. The image of the malls gets ruined by the presence of such people walking in. What would tourists say about our great country? It is like a soup where chicken is mixed with pieces of tasteless bones, eh? A line between layers of our society must be drawn clearly and well respected."

I could see how Gen liked to be the king of the table and have his theories accepted as facts. No wonder he was not beloved, but I couldn't see at that moment how that might be related to the bad feeling I kept getting in his presence.

"Hey, Gerald, my mother told me that your family name is Arsov?" He started again.

My eyes turned to the grandmother, who dropped her eyes to her plate, which was almost untouched.

"Yes," I replied.

"That sounds like a Russian name."

"I don't know why my father bore that strange surname." I smiled.

"Where is your father now?" Gen looked me in eyes.

"In Thailand," I lied. I didn't intend to give him the story of my life.

"What is he doing there?"

"Business."

"And your mother?"

"She always accompanies him wherever he goes. She is stuck to him like his tail." I chuckled.

At this point, the grandmother's expressions lightened as if she was waiting for my lies to be spoken. I didn't see any reason behind the interrogation.

"I used to know a family with the same surname." He spoke again.

"Arsov?" I enquired.

"Yes."

I forced my mouth to continue working on the piece of chicken and hide whatever signs of surprise his remark caused within me.

"I guess even Russian names can be copied." I smiled.

As I continued to eat, thoughts came to my mind. I realized that if he had really known a family with the same surname, it would have to be mine, especially in China. No coincidence could have brought another family with the same surname to China. But the big question was how he knew my family. It was unbearable to hold that question in my mind, and I looked up from my plate to ask it, only to see Gen standing and walking into the kitchen while licking his fingers. This wasn't the time for it.

I kept asking myself how a piece of garbage like Gen might have known my family. I knew father to be logical and respectful towards others. If that was the truth about my father, there would be no reason to keep in contact with such a hideous character as Gen. I couldn't see why Gen would joke about knowing my family, if he was really joking. His face didn't show any indication that he was a guy who would share casual jokes. The question of how he knew them was eating me up.

That day didn't satisfy my hunger for truth. When I went home, my mind was busy with the new thread that had emerged that was related to my parents, and I was wondering whether the bad feeling I kept getting in the presence of Gen was related to the secret information I was seeking. The following days did not help me with what I sought, though I caught glimpses of happiness when I was in contact with Li. I didn't wish to make it only a matter of sexual desires with her, because I truly carried feelings for her, and so I met her most days after her work at coffee shops or restaurants. She seemed to be very happy with me and was always in hurry to meet me, like a teenager who falls in love for the first time, and I do believe she fell in love with me. I liked her attitude of showing me care and pure kindness, and that made her even more special. She also would always send me text messages asking about me and whether I had my meals. I do believe she will make a fantastic wife once she is lucky with the right man. My destiny wasn't meant to be with her, and yet my heart longed for the promise of happiness she might provide me, and thus I wouldn't forgive myself for abandoning her.

One week after our first meeting, I invited Li for dinner in a small restaurant. As I was walking that evening to my destination, I stopped by a dress shop, as the dress on the glass window had caught my eye. The dress was similar to the one Li always wore in style, but the pink skirt was substituted with light oceanic blue. I imagined how it would look pretty on her. At first sight, I believed it was even the exact size for her. I stopped myself from following temptation and buying it for her; I didn't wish to create any sort of bonds of commitment she would believe in with me.

As I continued to stare at the dress, I saw a well-known complexion reflected in the glass, the beloved and much dreamed-of figure of Fang. The weak breezes of the sky blew her silky hair, making her fine face visible. I didn't turn around for fear of losing that view that always followed me within my dead memories. My heart dropped all its guards and wished for nothing more than just to look at her angel face. I let that figure in black dress pass by, and a black car with dark tinted windows stopped. The back door was opened by a man in a black suit, and the ghost of Fang climbed in. I realized now that I was losing her once again, if she was really Fang, and so I turned around quickly and ran towards the car, but my feet were not fast enough. The engine roared and the car sped away along the road. I paused there for a while unable to catch any more glimpses of the car. Then I thought about it over again. That girl couldn't be the Fang I knew, I told myself, or at least I just made myself believe it.

I turned and walked back to the new shiny girl in my life. I could see, by comparison, that I was ready to leave Li and everything for the sake of the first name my heart intuitively spoke—Fang.

26

When I was with Li, I always put thought into my dress; I liked to look good for her. Although my mind was totally against it, the quest of my heart demanded it. When I met her that evening, she had on her normal white and pink dress, and for a second I recalled the picture I had imagined of her wearing that blue dress. She had arrived before me, and her eyes were fixed on the young couple two tables away as they held hands and exchanged loving gestures. I paused for a while, thinking again about the effect I was having on her life and the effect she was actually wanting me to have over her life. Like a teenager, I approached her from behind and tapped her left shoulder, while turning around to take a seat on her right. She laughed when she saw me in front of her.

"I didn't know you were a guy who jokes." She smiled and leaned her head a little to the left. Her eyes were shining crystals under the yellow light of the room.

"Is it good if I joke?" I asked. It was the first time anyone had made such a comment.

"Yes, for sure." She straightened her head and placed her fingers around the glass of water in front of her. "You are just a very serious type, Gerald. I would like seeing you always laughing and joking. A smile looks good on your face."

"So be it. I shall change my skin."

She ordered chicken soup and so did I, and in the short period before the order was delivered, her eyes didn't stop stealing glimpses of the couple two tables away. Girls love to be loved and shown deeds of love. I am just a boring presence when it comes to anything related to love. The soup was placed on the table, and Li slowly moved her spoon around in it, stirring it in more than taking it to her mouth.

"What is it, Li?" I asked, seeing that she wasn't her normal self.

"Nothing . . . nothing." she replied, while her spoon kept moving around the soup bowl.

Silence dominated the air. I started to eat my soup. I didn't know what was wrong with her, and I couldn't see whether I had the right to investigate it. Sometimes women change their mood more frequently than they change their makeup and dress.

"You have not approached me since your visit to grandma's house." Li spoke almost in a whisper, and despite the tranquillity of the restaurant, I could barely hear her.

"Not approached you!" I looked at her, speaking softly. "Is that what you are upset about? We always meet, talk, and share thoughts."

"You must have so many girls in your life." Her eyes were still fixed on her soup bowl.

I couldn't see her point. Her words were riddles for me to connect.

"What are you talking about, Li? Please tell me what is going on in your mind."

"If you really don't have any other girl, you would ask me to your apartment . . . you would . . . sleep with me again after that first night." The tops of her cheeks reddened with blushes as she spoke those words.

Now things were clear to me. The fact that I had not been sleeping with her was, for her, a sign that I had other girls in my palace and that she was just a part-time toy to play with.

"I promise I have no other girl," I said, reaching out my hand and placing it on her cheek. I brushed her cheek with my thumb and then moved my hand to her tiny chin and pinched there gently. "But giving this promise doesn't mean that I am an ideal person. I have, like any man, a dark side to my life. It is only that I don't want to hurt you, Li, and don't want you to think of me as a guy who is just after your cunt."

She laughed and held my hand with both of hers and placed a gentle kiss on my palm.

"I am so sorry for bringing this silly little thought to our relationship," she murmured.

"I am happy you have spoken your heart."

We had our soup then while exchanging glimpses and smiles. Looking at her innocent face, I felt guilty for being with her for now and for planning for my life beyond her expectations.

"Listen to me." I looked at her seriously.

She swallowed what she had in mouth and opened her eyes with full attention.

"What if I was to marry you for less than a year, share life, love, and happiness with you, and then, say after ten months, leave you widowed where you can touch only the sand atop my grave."

My words fell heavily on her and on me as well. I had spoken very seriously with no glint in my eye.

"You are scaring me, Gerald." She attempted to smile but then dropped it, seeing my eyes fixed strongly and fiercely on her. "Yes. If you are seeking an answer, my answer is yes," she quietly said.

"It is not a joke. I am asking you. Answer me seriously from your heart," I demanded.

"Yes," she answered after a pause and with her eyes now wet. "I swear it to God. Every moment with you is a blessing for me, and if you are talking about living with me for ten months as a husband, that is a lifetime for me. Being widowed is not scary. Losing a beloved one is completely bitter, but if you fill me with lovely memories, I will grow old embracing them." She cleared her throat. "I don't know much about you, Gerald, and I am not interested in your past and your future plans. I am interested in your fidelity to me."

A wet drop scrolled to the end of her eye and fell onto her cheek. I wiped it clear. Our bowls were empty of soup. Our eyes met regularly in a silent manner and our mouths were shut. I realized she was thinking now of what would come of the words exchanged between us just a couple of minutes ago. I had my plan for her.

The couple two tables away were gone, and no one was there on our left except for a slightly tinted window that served as a mirror. Li's eyes were fixed there mostly, avoiding looking at me directly, but not avoiding looking at me through my reflection on the mirror. In her pure innocence, she didn't realize that I knew that she was looking at me. I pulled closer the embroidered napkin on the table, and still she didn't turn her head. I took a pen from my pocket and started writing on the napkin, but still she didn't turn her head. I folded the napkin and pushed it towards her, and now she responded and her eyes analysed the folded napkin for a while before unfolding it and reading my note. She covered her mouth with her hand and blushed in silent laughter.

"Okay," she said as she moved her hand to cover her eyes. Her perfectly straight white teeth were fascinating.

My note on the napkin read,

> Your mouth crystal and tits perfect and small,
> My tongue wishes on your vagina to roll.

It is surprising that such a dirty comment could have an uplifting effect on some girls. I guess everything is different when you are with somebody you carry real feelings for, and that was the case with Li and me.

Twenty minutes later Li was sitting on the small sofa in my apartment, legs spread, skirt and panties off, and my head buried in between her warm thighs, licking the flaming cunt and bringing feverish moans out of her. Her whole body trembled, ravished with a current that was spiking through it just three minutes after starting the activity. Her thighs started closing up in a shiver, squeezing my head, and she started to lift her flattened bottom. I wrapped my arms around her and carried her small body like a child. I placed her on my lap and shook her like a bottle of whisky. My fingers rubbed every piece of her golden body. She went through multiple orgasms, and her small body made failed attempts to free her from my clenched hands that were wrapped around her waist till I had my explosion. Li lay on the sofa and I on the floor, both out of breath. Her gasping was very deep, and she followed that with weak giggles, and so did I. I reached with my fingers after a while and started caressing her feet.

"I didn't dream of having sex with you," she laughed.

"You didn't?" I asked.

"Oh, yes," she giggled again. "Many times during college. You were my crush."

"And how was it in your dream?"

"Not as beautiful as it is in reality. You are amazing. You must have experienced many, many girls, right?"

That was a question I didn't wish to answer, not to her, and I tried to escape the subject.

"How is your father?" I asked, recalling the mystery of him knowing my family.

"No one knows." She was brushing the bottom of her foot on the thick hair of my chest.

"Where can I find him?"

"Why? He is not someone you should be with. No pure-hearted person would be with him."

Pure-hearted person! How good that description would make anyone feel. But was I? People who love you would make an angel or even God out of you. I was nothing close to that.

"I might change him after all," I commented.

"Change him!" she laughed. The tips of her feet fingers were smoothing my chest hair. "You cannot change a devil."

"A devil!" I was surprised at her harsh words about her own father.

"You don't know him. There is a rumour that he was the cause for the death of a family."

That sentence rang in my ears loudly, with a shock that cemented me where I was. Was Gen related in some way to the tragedy of my family? More thoughts started to flow in my mind, and confusion followed. I was much hungrier now for the truth about Gen's relationship to my family. I insisted that Li arrange a meeting between me and her father. She gave me his phone number but told me that I could find him in the Land Chrome night club almost every night.

Everything was soon to be uncovered, and I dearly sought the truth.

27

The next night, I visited Land Chrome. It was crowded and so loud that my mind started repeating the beats, and very expensive. I wondered whether all those people there had deep pockets. How many rich people are there in society? My eyes were unable to locate the thick-moustached Gen. I took my mobile phone and dialled his number, but the signal wasn't strong enough there to carry my call.

Not so far away girls were dancing around posts on a round stage, bra-less, but neither those girls nor all the lesbians kissing in the club moved me a bit. I had a purpose beyond sex now, and nothing would help but satisfying it. Some girls touched and grabbed my ass. I cannot confirm whether it was done intentionally, but I didn't mind it. Some heels and heavy shoes stepped on my feet as I moved among the crowd, and one drunk girl crashed against my body, spilling the wine in her glass all over me. She grabbed the bottom of my T-shirt and tried to pull it up, asking me to undress. I just pushed her to the floor and walked away. I dialled Gen's number again, and still the signal was weak. Didn't those people complain about such bad service in a luxurious bar like that, I wondered.

In one corner of the bar, there was mad chattering that was attracting attention. I walked over there and stole a glimpse at what was going on. To my surprise, all those men and women were gathered around a rectangular table, on top of which a naked muscular man was enjoying himself having sex with a naked blond girl, who was covered in perspiration. I was filled immediately with disgust for those shallow people gathered there to witness one of the bitter shames of life's mockery. A free live porn for all who would like to watch!

My eyes went to a couple in the front line of the crowd just behind the table, who kept looking at the sex scene and smiling and whispering to each other, with the man's hand patting and brushing the girl's hips. Within a minute or so, the girl separated from her partner and walked to the table. She approached the moaning girl on the table and started sucking her wet breasts and hard nipples. In a second the new girl was out her clothes, and, shockingly, the guy had his sex rage on both the half-done girl and the new vigorous girl. The chattering of the crowd grew louder and deeper.

I stood with the crowd of sinners and watched that hard sex performance. Nothing there attracted me to stay, but I stayed because the man I was looking for was in front of me, fully naked, the hero of the scene. Even if the signal was good in the bar that night, how would an involved busy man like him allow his mobile phone to distract him from the ultimate pleasure he was having in public? When you bury your shame so deep in the filth, nothing you do would be perceived so bad. That man, the father of a lovely daughter, allowed himself to be swallowed in dirt, without thinking what damage it might bring to his daughter's reputation. I believed Li now: her father was a devil, and I believed now that this guy would be capable of doing any wrong towards others, and my parents might not been an exception.

Gen finished with a loud orgasm, while I guess the other two girls might have been done much earlier. He was gasping heavily now. The crowd started applauding, whistling, and chanting encouraging words for the devilish man who had provided them with the stimulating delight of their night. He wiped himself up with the roll of tissues that one of the attendees placed on the table. Then, leaving the heap of tissues behind, Gen put on his underwear, jeans, and T-shirt.

"Your drink is on me," I said loudly and managed to catch his attention.

He was doing up his belt when he turned. He gave a look of surprise, and the proud smile half faded from his face.

"Where is Li?" Gen asked, his hands slowly finishing the belt.

"Li? Oh, no, she is not here with me."

His proud smile returned to his face. A drop of perspiration was moving down the left side of his head.

"My drink is on you, you say."

"Yes."

He moved towards me and reached out his hand. I hesitated for a while whether to shake his hand, the hand that was used for shit and clearly unwashed. But I did shake hands with him in the end, seeing that as a step to create confidence between us. We sat and I ordered him a drink. The table was round and so very small that I had to sit on one side and pull my legs out from under it, but that positioning didn't stop his unpleasing body odour from reaching my nose.

"Wine is the water for the soil of the soul," he giggled with a gasp.

Gen kept drinking and talking rubbish as usual. He even talked about his sex scene in the way one would talk about sport or any casual news—that he couldn't control himself seeing that young girl, the most beautiful stripper in the bar, and that she got all everything in his pocket to convince her to participate in a public sex scene with him. I let him talk and talk and ordered him glass after glass. After twenty minutes, he was drunk and was murmuring more disconnected rubbish and laughing aloud with a creaky sound that made others around our table laugh. The tough guy who had just showed others his sexual prowess was no more than a silly joke now.

"Did you really know the Arsov family?" I asked, seeing that the time was suitable to bring out his secret.

"Arsov? Ooh, yeah. One more drink," He reached out his hand.

I ordered him one more glass and took it in my hand.

"Try to answer my question to get this." I lifted my hand, holding the glass above my head. Like a hungry dog, he stretched his unbalanced hands to catch it.

"Ask me again." He spoke with a hiccup.

"How did you know of the Arsov family?"

"That damn family . . . that ruined family . . ." He took the glass from my hand and took a small sip. A long pause followed, making me think he wouldn't continue talking.

"Talk," I said in a hard demanding tone.

"Just wait . . . trying to re-taste the sweet memory of Huan." His mouth opened with a smelly smile.

Huan! He had mentioned my mother's name. Now I had a really bad feeling and could recognize his evil influence on my family. Now I could see the reason behind the strange feeling I had experienced when I first saw his picture in his mother's home.

"I met that lady in a restaurant, and we talked casually, but she never got over that one meeting. She started coming to the same restaurant again and again to meet me. I am a handsome rich man, you see." He rubbed his palms on the edge of the table. "I took her from there and shared casual sex with her day after day. I nailed her the way I nailed Li's mother. You see, girls are whores by nature, and you should be dominating the business."

My inner self was in turbulence. I wiped my mouth continuously with my shaking hand and tried hard to control that waking vigour that raged within me. I didn't know my mother well, and I couldn't say where Gen stood in her life or whether he was the only side partner she had.

"Didn't you know she was married?" I questioned in an unbalanced tone.

"Married! What girl is not married and seeks fun? But yes, technically, Huan was married, although she denied it initially. Women seek dicks, and the best in town was mine." He laughed loudly. "I knew later that she was married, but I wasn't going to stop grapping something so very convenient. My joy in life is sex. Sex gives meaning to manhood. Isn't that right?"

"What about her children," I commented.

"She didn't have any. She said her one child died at birth."

Died at birth! How cruel but how realistic, if my mother had indeed said it. She considered me dead. Why do such mothers give birth to curses that they themselves curse? People like me are just time bombs whose explosion might bring destruction to others as well. And I was about to explode in Gen's face with punches loaded with my heavily armed anger and rage. I had unexpectedly found out the murderer of my parents, when all I was seeking was a peaceful death at the end of my due time. Tears rolled in my eyes for a reason I couldn't perceive. I hated my mother even more now. I hated my father. I hated most of all that sack of sinful dirt sitting in front of me with his hands smelling of loathsome sperm.

"Will you order me one more glass now?" He opened his mouth and burped.

I put my hand around the glass on the table and held it tight. I felt dizzy, and things were starting to get blurry in my eyes. I didn't wish to leave him just like that. I wished to make him drink from the glass of agony from which I had been fed for years and years. My hand uncontrollably pressed tighter around the glass, and within a minute a small voice followed. I was alarmed to look at my hand to see it covered in blood and shattered pieces of glass. Nobody seemed to notice. Only the waitress with tightly pushed-up breasts, who approached with another unordered glass of wine, covered her mouth with her free hand and screamed. Different thoughts came into my mind. I was now the centre of attention as a couple of people started asking me whether everything was all right. I was forced to flee the whole scene, but it seemed like a big failure on my part. The thought came to my mind that I might not be able to meet Gen again. What if he died today and I couldn't avenge myself, I thought. I was allowed to escape. I stood, but felt my feet were failing me. The smile on Gen's face was because he was drunk, but it disgusted me like nothing else. I dug my way out of the crowd as drops of blood dropped on the floor and stained some of the people when my hand brushed against them. Outside the night club, just after passing the big guard, I stepped to one side and threw up. The guard asked me, frightened, whether something wrong had happened to me. I waved him off.

I couldn't sleep that night. I could see how bad my mother was for the hideous decision she made to cheat on my father. But nothing mattered now about my parents. I couldn't question their wrong-doing, I could just hate them and blame them. I would be dying soon, and all the loathing I felt for them would be over. But the annoying thing was to know that the person who directly or indirectly contributed to the ruin of my family was still breathing, eating and drinking, and enjoying life more than many others, despite his knowledge of the tragedy he brought upon my family. My anger was directed towards Gen more than my parents and more than my life that I detested. I felt that I must do something—something really bad.

The idea came to mind of murdering Gen. That would be the only way, I felt, I could feed that rising anger in me. It would be, I believed, the ultimate well-deserved end of a devil who mocked the lives of others and cared about nothing but his own lust. It is true that my mother wasn't ideal, that she didn't love me, that she was full of deception, and that she did deserve to die. I cannot deny it. But the fires of hell had not yet consumed the architect of the situation. He was still living, weighing heavily on my chest, wallowing in whatever joy he could attain, while it was I who had suffered the whole of my life, thinking and planning my own death and sipping any tiny portion of happiness that was offered to ease this always-hurting heart of mine. Yes, I thought, I had to put an end to it. The fire that had consumed those two should swallow all involved. Gen and I were the two survivors. My death was waiting down the line, I thought, but it was troubling to look at Gen without being able to read his expiration date.

The next morning I felt sick and lacked energy, but I would allow nothing to stand in the path I had decided to follow. I went outside, and all the smells of food coming from homes and restaurants filled me with nausea. In a nearby supermarket I bought bananas, strawberries, honey, and fresh milk. I went back home, and there was a text message from Li on my mobile phone. She asked about me and whether we could meet in the afternoon. I replied that I had something urgent to handle, without mentioning any details. I knew that she would think about my answer later and question me when we met. I mixed the stuff I bought into the mixer and had my juice. After an hour of reading, I did some exercise. Then I worked on my book, *The Way to Suicide*.

I was back at Land Chrome the next night. My heart was thumping against my chest. I was going to a murder scene, I thought, completely unprepared for the crime I was going to commit. Once I was inside the club, I checked around and looked for Gen, but there was no sign of him anywhere. I asked some of the people I had seen there the day before, but they denied seeing him that night. I picked up my mobile phone and dialled his number, but the damn signal was yet weak. After half an hour waiting, I went out of the club and dialled his number again, but the phone now seemed to be switched off.

I was very irritated and upset about my bad luck, and I felt totally uncomfortable once I was out on the street. I dialled Li's number. She answered sweetly, and we agreed to meet although it was almost eleven and she had duty the next day. She was my true shelter and what I asked for.

"You look sick," she commented, examining my face and touching my forehead.

"Do I?"

"Are you sick?" she asked.

I smiled at her innocence and held her hand. "No, dear, just tired," I said.

"What was keeping you busy tonight?"

We walked side by side and sat on a bench. The street lamp was above us, and even though its light was weak, it was enough to illuminate Li's face and bring out, for my pleasure, all her lovely expressions.

"I had to attend a friend of mine who is sick."

"A friend?" She waited to know the gender.

"A male friend."

For a moment, I thought how we would be together once we were married. My freedom would be sweetly caged, with the keys around her neck. We sat on the bench for about an hour, and she talked about her working day, her office mates and their internal love affairs, and her manager and his hated bossy attitude. Eventually we separated with a kiss on cheek from my side that didn't have the capacity to satisfy her and was doubled by a kiss on lips. I managed that night to conceal my bandaged hand from her. I already felt guilty about the lie I had told. I didn't wish to add more on it.

The following night the murderer inside me was back to Land Chrome. I spotted Gen that night, and my heart beat more heavily. He was sharing a table with an ugly woman whose hair was a mix of red, light brown, and black colours. Her eyebrows were thicker than what is pleasing to see in a woman. I approached the table and greeted Gen. The woman—a cheap prostitute, I guess—looked me over.

"Your son?" she asked Gen.

"No, no," he laughed. "The boyfriend of my daughter."

"Lucky her," she commented, and she walked away from the table as she read Gen's hand signal to do so.

He asked me to have a seat and shook hands with me.

"How is she?" He asked, waving to a waitress to come.

"Who?" I wondered.

"Sorry, Li, I mean." He ordered me and himself a drink.

"Best as ever, happy as never," I replied.

"The girl loves you," he added.

"She told you that?"

"One can see that clearly."

The waitress came back with the drinks. Gen paid her and spanked her butt as she walked away, a gesture that brought a slutty noise out of her. I put both my hands on the table and held the glass with them. For a second, I thought of breaking that glass and slashing his throat.

"Have you injured yourself?"

"It is nothing," I waved my hand. I was waiting for him to say something about the glass I had broken the day before yesterday in his presence, but I could see that Gen was unable to recall anything since he had been under the heavy influence of alcohol.

"You are not participating in any of the acts tonight?" I asked, pointing to the corner where he held his sex scene the last time.

He giggled and crossed his hands behind his head. "Not if I am not provoked to. It requires daring and physical strength, you know."

And stupidity, I thought. "Where were you yesterday?" I asked.

"Come, let's go on the roof. The weather is wonderful today." He spoke as if he hadn't heard my question.

He stood and swallowed his drink fast, and then he went to the counter and bought a bottle of wine. I followed him as he walked to the back of the bar, where behind a door was hidden a staircase leading up. As we opened the roof door, fresh air brushed our faces.

"Hmm." Gen murmured and sniffed while closing his eyes. "Everything in life seems wonderful when you rise, even just once, above the animal in you."

He sat on the slightly rough surface of the roof, and I sat opposite him. He removed the top of the bottle and threw it off the roof.

"I was busy yesterday, son."

His voice seemed lighter than I had ever heard him talk before. There was no arrogance. He hadn't forgotten my earlier question; he was just carrying it there with him. But how much I hated him calling me "son"!

"I had to lend a hand to a family whose life seemed to come to a total halt after the death of their breadwinner." He took a deep sip out of the bottle.

"You know the family?" I asked.

"The father was working in my sugar refinery factory. He committed suicide the day before yesterday because of his heavy unpaid loans that he couldn't pay with the creditors always on his tail." He sighed. "I had to ease the burden on the shoulders of his wife and youngsters." He took a big sip again. I felt for a second that he would be emptying the bottle with two more sips of the same size.

"He committed suicide?"

"People make decisions sometimes out of mental weakness, but it is still a decision they make, and it is their own decision."

"And you helped the family! What are you, a Santa Claus?" It was very hard to digest what he was saying.

He giggled. "Hard to believe, isn't it? I guess you've heard enough about me from Li. We may look hard, but we are human after all. Yes, I have made wrong decisions throughout my life, but part of me still cries when I'm alone. I long to see Li's mother now, but I am bearing the results of the decision I made to separate from her."

I kept silent and looked off the roof. The car park below seemed very peaceful and tranquil. Breezes were blowing from the east, not as gentle as the smell they brought with them, but gentle in their own right. Gen was feeling cold, I could see. He kept patting his arms and blowing on his palms.

"If I fall down drunk, take me home, son." He coughed and blew out a spit on his left. Then he mentioned his home address.

"Sure," I said, watching him shiver like a hen. I didn't really listen totally to his home address.

He might be a good person inside, I thought, but my anger towards him still lingered in my heart for what he had done. He might have reached out a kind hand to thousands, but to me he was a devil who ought to come to extinction. He started drinking more heavily and murmuring a mixture of words that would have made no sense to any rational person. My inner self trembled as I looked at him with hard eyes filled with the lust for revenge. The image of my father appeared in front of me holding the heart of my mother, and a sudden craving emerged with it for a loving warm parental hug. My parents might still have lived together. They might not always be fully happy, but no couple can live happy together for a lifetime. There are always ups and downs in a marriage.

To hell with all the kind deeds Gen might have done!. Who would give a damn if a murderer distributed flowers? I couldn't allow myself to believe in Gen's alleged kindness to others. I might have enjoyed that warm hug from my parents if Gen had not been introduced in their path.

He started to mumble, giggle, and sing some old song, and he was moving his hands and shoulders in a weird dance. I stood and looked over the edge of the roof. A noisy plane was lighting up the sky, which apart from the plane seemed so clear and pure. Tiny stars and a half moon were adding touches of beauty to the dark garment of the night. I took a deep breath. The cold air caressed my throat and lungs and brushed a wet layer on the surface of my eyes. I looked down off the roof. The asphalt was clear and clean.

"Gen, Gen," I shouted to catch his attention. "Come over here. See how this couple are having sex." I feigned a surprised look pointing down off the roof.

From the side of my eyes, I watched Gen push himself up and stand with difficulty. He wobbled with the few steps he took and stood next to me. He smelled bad again. I guess it was the result of the bad chemistry his body emitted when mixed with alcohol. He narrowed his eyes and pushed his chin ahead.

"Where?" he asked, and he trembled as his body's weight shifted to one foot and then back onto both feet.

I took a step or two back and saw him standing there in front of me. He took another sip from his bottle and placed it on the edge of the wall and then leant on the wall with his palms. The wall of the roof came up just to his hips, and Gen started to lean forward carelessly. But he wouldn't just fall and grant my wish to see him dead. I couldn't imagine him dying so easily of purely natural causes.

My hand reached out shaking towards his back, and my ears could hear only bubbles coming out of his mouth. My head was busy with things I cannot recall now, but my heart was empty of any real pettiness. It took me one gentle hesitating tap on his upper back to make him tremble and flip over the roof. How fragile he was despite his fit body! The sound of low laughter came to my ears, but soon it started fading into a long gasp. No further sound came but the crash of the body turning into a corpse as it collided with the ground. I looked over now, and for the first time the real image of that dark red blood sparkled in my eyes as well as on the ground, where it was lit up by the post lights.

I spotted a middle-aged man approaching the bar with his hand around the shoulders of a very young girl. The white bushy hair of the former and the silky black hair of the latter were a bad combination. They looked like a couple that I would have expected to be father and daughter, but as I stared, they didn't seem to share the sacred bonds of parenthood. The old man started reaching his hand down the chest of the girl and rubbing it there. The young girl sat on the pavement, or she was asked to do so, to be exact. Then she released a small scream as she caught sight of Gen's corpse. The old man, alarmed, turned his head, gave a look at the corpse, and then turned back to the girl whispering. The whispering turned within a couple of seconds to real sex, with the corpse lying just a few steps away and the blood trickling out in a slow thin river.

I turned back. My head was heavy. I walked quickly to the narrow door of the roof and went slowly down the steps. The colourful area of the night club disturbed my eyes and hurt my vision, but I tried to keep my composure as I walked out of the club. Once I was steps away, I added picked up speed and kept going from one narrow road to another. In the end I was lost and couldn't see where I exactly was. At one corner I paused and let out a rush of vomit. I felt cold all of a sudden, and I crossed my arms to fight it and kept walking. In a dirty dim-lit narrow street I let my body crawl down the wall and take rest there. I closed my eyes. My ears listened to the abnormal motion of my heart. I don't know for how long I was unconscious of time. Eventually there was a tap on my bent knee. I opened my eyes slightly to meet the darkness of the area, and then the figure of a girl started forming on my left.

"Hey," she said repeatedly till our eyes met. "Are you drunk?"

I shook my head.

"Do you carry any money?"

I raised my eyebrow but didn't answer.

"I can give you a quick blowjob for any amount you can offer."

I raised my head a little and met her partially covered chest. My nose was disturbed by the heavy cheap perfumed lotion she had on. I instantly realized she was a prostitute.

"You can help me take a taxi. I will pay you."

I provided her my home address and she disappeared for a couple of minutes to come back shouting that a cab was waiting. She helped me to stand, and I thanked her as we walked. As I entered the cab, I pushed some amount of money into her hand without realizing how much.

Unknown fear was dominating me all over. In my dark room, I buried my head under the pillow and shut my eyes tight.

28

$\mathcal{M}$y cell phone kept ringing continuously. I reached out and searched for the source of the noise, only to find it at last in my pocket. Without looking at the caller, I answered, and Li's voice came from the other end, sad and thick.

"My father is dead," she said and then wept.

Memories of the previous night flooded back into my mind.

"Is . . . is he?" came out my mouth unconsciously.

"Yes," she said. She told me about the funeral arrangements and asked me to attend.

I recognized myself now as a murderer, but I wouldn't reveal it to her, not in my life. My heart was squeezing in my chest, and I could see that I had lost all sense of life and beauty around me. I couldn't eat that whole day, and yet I was determined to attend the funeral the next day to satisfy Li. I wished to keep my strength as long as possible, but the knowledge that you are a murderer is as hot as burning in hell.

I swallowed some fruit that I found in the fridge, but I threw it up later in the toilet in the form of thick liquid. I wasn't guilty of committing that crime, and neither am I now. I believe it was the right fate for Gen; his crime against my family was punished, and he had forfeited his life. But the heart is weak, and that feeling of having stolen the right to exist from someone troubled me. When you kill someone, you kill his future and put an end to all his unachieved dreams and planned deeds.

At the funeral, my face wasn't the only strange face. There was a variety of different nationalities. I saw how influential Gen had been. My eyes could barely meet anybody else's, knowing that I was the murderer of the man whose funeral it was. As soon as she saw me, Li walked fast towards me and wrapped me in a tight embrace. I admit now, as I recall her in that black garment, that she looked even more beautiful than ever, but I couldn't see her beauty at the time. I attempted to put my hands on her back to return the embrace, but my hands were shaking. I am a criminal. I lowered my hands back to my sides. All of a sudden, the grandma appeared. She stopped when she saw me and threw me an angry glare. When Li opened her hands around me, the grandma was gone.

"It is okay," I said with a smile. Her eyes were red with tears.

The funeral functions went on, and I preferred to stay alone, away from the crowd. At one point, the grandmother was just in front of me. I winced at the sight of her grim face.

"Have you had your revenge on us now?" she asked in a creaking voice.

I wondered for a while what she was implying, but then I realized she knew about my crime.

"Yes." I looked at my shoes and then turned my eyes back on her in a challenging manner.

"Leave us know. Leave Li and go away."

Looking past her short figure, I caught sight of Li talking to another girl. I would miss her, I thought, and I would bring great sadness and depression on her. I apologized to her in my heart and walked out, dropping my cell phone in the nearest garbage bin. At that moment we separated forever. At that moment I gave her one more wrong perception about love and trust.

Less than five months now remained out there for me, and yet I was fading earlier. I had lost more than five kilograms and was not at all in good shape. Coughing accompanied me always, sometimes in a strong way. I thought many times of killing myself early, but something inside prevented me, telling me to wait a little longer. I listened to that tiny voice for the sake of the promise I had made to myself to die when I was twenty-nine. But for whatever illness or defects I got, I wouldn't seek any treatment. If my life was to stop at some point, I thought, I wouldn't interfere by putting it back on track.

I was abandoned, and I realized what an insignificant shadow I was. Loneliness never weighed as heavily on me as it did at that moment, and my confidence had never been weaker. It is when you need care that you discover your weaknesses. How different am I from my father! I guess I am like him for having a crime imprinted on my hands. We both committed a crime to satisfy our idea of vengeance. I am a criminal on the loose. My belief that I was a mistake of life grew even stronger.

29

One Friday morning I woke up to a violent coughing session. I felt myself dying, suffocating, to be honest, as less air circulated in my lungs. My chest was horribly painful as I tried to inhale deeply. Only the initial process of inhaling was possible without agony. I sat up sharply on my bed, my eyes illuminated by the view of the sun through the dust-tinted window. Though the young sun was just waking up as it first rose over the horizon, even in its weakness it burned my eyes. I closed them tight and lowered my face, with my hands clenched to my chest. Slowly, the pain started fading away. How much I hated living!

I didn't wish to wake up, but sleeping wasn't any more peaceful. Nightmares always distracted me from enjoying any tranquillity with myself. I could see and feel only death. My soul was full of bruises, so that I believed no remedy could redeem its tranquillity. All the ambitions that I had enjoyed quenching my lust upon had been melted and flattened to the ground. No sky beheld me anymore; earth overwhelmed me with its graves. It is not about all great things you do in life. It is whether all the things you do can bring you true happiness.

That morning, after a long time rolling around sleepless in bed, I went to a nearby park to sniff in some fresh air. The park was empty of all but a few people jogging, all of who were elderly, and a couple holding hands on a small bench, looking at the blue sky without speaking but with a smile on their faces. A group of birds suddenly appeared in the sky and landed in the park in beautiful accord. They spread out across from where I was sitting on my bench, picked out with their beaks whatever they sought, and then, unlike the form in which they landed, they flew away in arbitrary order.

I lowered my head, feeling far more relaxed than I had at home, and I closed my eyes. All my swollen memories were gone now, and tranquillity captured me with its rapture. I felt that I was dying in such peace that surrounded all my senses.

But then loud noises suddenly disturbed everything and blew away my feeling of peace. I opened my eyes to see a group of people, three males and one female. I was upset with the loud conversation they were having, disturbing my wonderland. Two of the males were helping each other with the video camera, which was focused on the other male figure, whose muscular body was caressing the girl, whose hair was beautifully highlighted. They were shooting some sort of movie, I guessed, and I was about to leave the scene when the face of the muscular guy stopped me.

"Bojing!" I said to myself.

I couldn't believe my eyes. He had a bigger figure than the person I remembered, and his face, which had once borne some pimples, was so clear and shiny now. Just to confirm it to myself, I said his name out loud, and he turned to me.

"Gerald! It cannot be. Gerald!" He left the girl and walked to me. He shook my hand hard.

"Oh, no, not again, Bojing." The camera men sighed and lowered the camera and murmured something to each other, pointing at Bojing.

"Just wait, guys." Bojing said. "He is my best friend, and we haven't seen each other for years, don't you see that?" Then he turned to me again. "I am sorry, Gerald. I have to finish this movie. Shall we meet again?"

I nodded with a big smile.

"Can I have your number?" he asked.

"I don't have any cell phone. I was about to buy one." The latter statement was a lie.

"You take mine." He pulled out a small piece of paper from his pocket and borrowed, without permission, a pen from the top pocket of one of the camera men. He handed me the paper. "Call me today, tonight, any time." He tapped on my shoulder and waved to the cameramen to resume shooting, while he took his position with the girl.

The shooting resumed. Bojing's hand rubbed the girl's back and then slowly went down on the top of her ass. The girl tittered, or just acted so. They all went out through the gate of the park, where a small van was awaiting them. I don't think that I ever considered Bojing as a best, or even a close, friend, but I was truly happy for him that he had become an actor.

I went and bought myself a new cell phone and a SIM card. I waited till evening, sitting on my bed doing nothing but looking through the window, having had only a piece of croissant and hot chocolate the whole day. At the first sign of dusk, I took the piece of paper from my pocket where the number was written. I turned it over and found it a supermarket receipt. I dialled the number, and it was instantly answered. He asked me to meet him in a seafood restaurant, giving me the address.

Within two hours we were having baked squid.

"This beard of yours and the black marks under your eyes . . . you look different. You've lost weight also, haven't you?" Bojing said.

"Life wasn't so loyal to me," I simply replied.

He licked his thumb and then picked another piece of squid. "You know you can come to me for any assistance or help."

"You have gained more muscles, I see, and . . . wow, you are an actor. You seem to have reached your dreams." I smiled and opened my eyes wider with a surprised expression.

"I have been training harder and eating more. It is my job requirement." He adjusted himself on the chair and gave a quick glance to his left. His eyes were looking down, and there was a slight pale shadow of unease on his face. "An actor, yes." His voice dropped all of sudden. "I am a porn star, Gerald." My gaze was still on him, but the smile on my face faded away at this news. "Life wasn't so loyal to me either. I have worked harder

244

and harder, but no future has seemed to approach my dreams. Any agency that approached me for a modelling audition offered me a very low income." He swallowed and brushed the edge of the table with the tips of his fingers. "Well, I am making enough in this business, and it is spreading wide all over the world."

A moment of cautious silence fell between us. I thought of the business Bojing was involved in. What sort of opportunities might it offer and what future lay ahead for him?

"But still you are an actor," I said, and I giggled trying to give him some encouragement, even though I didn't really agree. "Who has the right to judge whether it is right or wrong!"

He looked at me and faked a giggle. I could see the spark revive in his eyes, and his usual smile reappeared on his lips.

"You wouldn't believe it, Gerald, the sort of girls who take part in this business with their full consent. Many are so young and so cute that you, I believe, would feel terrible seeing them getting fucked for cash. It is such a strange business. The world is very shallow about money, you see."

I don't know whether he realized that he himself fell perfectly into that category of cash-shallow people.

"How many holes have you tried so far in the job?" I asked jokingly.

"How many holes? Mm, I guess fifteen in total with ten girls. You got me, right?"

"Have you enjoyed them?"

"I am gay, you know. I don't enjoy sex with females."

"Do they know about it?"

"Me being gay? Why, should they? I'd prefer to fake heterosexuality and nail females than show my true form and get pounded repeatedly by unworthy males."

I laughed. "What was that shooting this morning?"

"Every porn movie has a starter, an opening that prepares the viewer for what is coming next, and that was what we were doing this morning. The girl is hot, isn't she? She asked me about you and mentioned that you are handsome. She was thinking you are a porn star as well, but I denied it. You could work as a porn star, Gerald. Did you know that? Though you look a bit sick now, your complexion still retains its charm."

"No, no, no," I waved my hand. "It is not for me, this whole business."

"Just if you are in need of some quick cash, if you get what I mean."

"And then be spotted on the street as a porn worker?" I laughed and ran my hand through my hair.

"Why? There are dozens of people who look like you and me. That is the nature of the world. Normally people will not point fingers at others; accusing some stranger is so risky."

"Still, no. My answer is no . . ."

His cell phone rang and he answered it, walking away from the table. He returned within minutes.

"They are asking me to participate in a small sex video tonight." He looked at his watch, "I need to go, as shooting will start within two hours. Do you want to be a viewer tonight for a live porn scene?"

I shook my head and stood up from the chair ready to leave.

"Please, do join me. You need to see all forms of people to realize the nature of the world we live in. You need to witness with your eyes the things you see as wrong before you judge them so."

I hesitated and then agreed. He was right in what he said. We walked for a while, and then he stopped a taxi.

"There is this girl, mmm . . . your college classmate, I guess, who used to follow you. She is the one I am going to fuck tonight." He talked loud to overcome the high volume music the driver was playing.

"A classmate of mine!" I wondered. During my time in college so many girls had been after me.

"Anyway, you will meet her soon."

The cab stopped and we got out.

"It is there, the shooting of the clip." He pointed to a blue house. "So many shootings take place there. It is a regular home, isn't it? You cannot differentiate it from any other house in the neighbourhood. Some closed doors conceal sinful secrets, you see."

I didn't comment. I was really curious to know what was going on in there, though I wasn't a bit happy about it.

"Over a year I have worked in this business. Some nights I just wonder whether I am one of the reasons to spoil the innocent lives of these young girls working in this business."

I looked at him. His eyes were cast down, and his eyebrows were close to the eyelids in a deep thoughtful expression.

"Do you remember in college when we used to watch porn movies?" he asked.

I nodded, but I wasn't sure that he noticed.

"We used to enjoy them a lot," he continued. "Every single guy would enjoy watching porn. But now I see how some young girls put their pure innocence on the line and what they agree to go through for the sake of satisfying their un-tamed lust for cash. What are our parents made of? Why do they give life hideous worms that eat up its beauty?"

I kept silent again. He had given things much thought, and yet he was still working in porn. I didn't wish to give him any personal advice in the matter. I wasn't in any position to do so. I am a murderer and he is a killer of innocence.

We reached the house, and Bojing wiped his eyes clear with the backs of his fingers before ringing the door bell. A middle-aged man opened the door, and Bojing shook hands with him. The man asked about me, and Bojing told him a lie that I was a new porn worker looking to gain experience by watching. We were welcomed in. Bojing whispered to me that the man was the owner of the house, renting it some nights secretly for porn filming. He asked me then to keep silent and to walk without making any noise as it might disturb the other rooms.

All the rooms had closed doors except for one. I peeked in as I passed. A young woman had her back laid on the top of the man under her, while another muscular man was on top of her, having her from the front. It was a very seductive scene, with the girl in pain and her skin laminated with a brush of sweat. The woman's mouth kept opening and closing like a fish, while her feet, having lost their space on the floor, were dangling in the air as the two monsters pounded her hard. All of sudden, her eyes caught me standing unaware. The cameraman's eyes followed, and he waved to one of the crew to close the door. I walked away and then looked back to see the door closed. We were now in the living room, where a group of girls, most of them nicely dressed like normal teens, were scattered across the colourful sofas, talking and chattering to each other. They all turned at me as soon as one of them pointed and moved her eyes towards me. We stood for a while there as Bojing made a call to the person who had invited him.

"Who are you?" one jolly teenager asked me.

I looked at her and let my eyes wander across the other girls. I ignored the question. I knew they were waiting for their turn. Some were very young to be working in porn, judging from their almost flat chests. Bojing went out of the living room through another opening at our back. I went to follow him, when a piece of cloth flew through the air towards me. I reached out my hand and grabbed it; it was a pair of tiny T-back panties that would fit a doll. Laughter followed. I stared at the girls.

"What is your name, handsome?"

I didn't know who had asked the question. I squeezed the panties in my hand and then dropped them on the floor, before going through the opening at my back. I looked left and right, but there was no sign of Bojing. There were six doors, three on each side of the corridor I was standing in, with all the doors closed. The pinkish-red rug under my feet was gloomy, and what made it worse were the two dim yellow lights at each end of the corridor. The owner of the house ought to be rich, I believed, and yet he was renting his house to assist in creating a generation of true young prostitutes. It is very difficult to overcome greed.

I waited for a minute, but Bojing seemed to have started his work, forgetting or losing me. I knew he was in one of the six rooms, but searching for him wasn't an option. What attracted me were the pictures hanging on the wall on the left of each of the six doors. I was about to leave, but curiosity pushed me to look at the pictures. I walked to each of the picture on my left and right till I reached the last; they all showed clowns in action, nicely painted. They told of the mockery of life. While some clowns are on ladders working hard to build one half of the unfinished home, the other clown is smoking a cigar in an armchair in the painted and furnished part. While one clown, wearing dirty torn clothes, is sitting on the roof watching stars with a dreamy expression, the other clown, dressed in gold, is treading the earth with an expression of arrogance. They were such captivating pictures. It was worth studying them, but I wondered if the owner of the house or any of the people working there had done so! I reached the last picture—one clown eating the flesh of another. I examined the picture and gave some thought to what it might imply. It was the strangest of all of them. The door behind me opened, disturbing my meditation. Some light was let out of the room into the darkness of the corridor. A man walked out silently, not noticing me and me not giving any attention to him. The door was left open behind him.

In the reflection on the glass of the framed picture in front of me, a shirtless guy's figure was moving, I recognized it as Bojing, and so I decided to stay where I was and watch a fragment of Bojing's scene through the clown's picture. He had a smile on his face while his left hand was playing with his groin. Then came something that shattered my eyes; I saw the lean figure of a girl that my mind instantly linked to a page of fond memories. My heart drummed hard. I refused to look back at the reality the reflection might be showing. Bojing reached his hand out and placed it on the girl's cheek, which he brushed with the back of his fingers. I didn't want to believe it. I thought it was just some game my imagination was playing that would fade away with a single blink of my eyes. When I opened them again, the female figure was still standing, out of her one-part dress, with only the black bra and panties on, and Bojing was caressing the top of her shoulders.

What I was seeing in my sore eyes was so painful. My state of mind was in confusion. How could such a good girl choose such a dirty path? Bojing started to push the elastic straps of the bra down her shoulders, and all my nerves jumped in a sharp alarm. I turned my face now. My top layer of teeth was grinding against the lower. My fists were held so tight that my nails pierced through my palms, and eyes were burning with tears of anger. The black bra dropped to the floor, and I raised my eyes to see the girl's bare chest. Bojing's hand moved up towards her breasts, and at the same instant my feet pushed me and my body was flying off the ground and landing in the room, bringing shocked noises from everyone there, except for Fang, who gazed at me with silent calm eyes. The question pounded in my mind, why?

A hand grabbed at me. My mind, confused by all the noise, triggered a defensive signal, and my fist punched in the direction of the supposed threat. Bojing fell to the floor, and I grabbed Fang by her shoulders.

"Why?" I screamed in her face.

"Gerald," she spoke quietly, unaware of my loud voice and anger.

The cameramen were about to jump on me while hurling insults and bad words at me, but Bojing stopped them and scolded them. I could see something different about Fang. Her mind didn't seem to be aware of the reality of what was going on around her. I just wouldn't leave her there, at whatever cost. Picking her dress off the floor, I wrapped it around her top and, wrapping my arms around her shoulders, I dragged her out.

"I knew she is special to you. She kept repeating your name," Bojing said.

I ignored him, and I ignored all the curious male and female eyes in the house. I ignored the people in the road, ignored the surprised look on the taxi-driver's face, and I ignored life. She came quietly into my arms and rested her head on my chest. For a while I forgot where I had found her and my unanswered questions about the path she had followed. I lost the person I was. I was with the one person my heart desired. I was in the company of my one real love.

30

$\mathcal{I}$t was a small stolen pleasure just to think that I had gained what my heart secretly sought. Everything in my mind just ceased to exist except for my consciousness of the presence of Fang. I opened the door of my apartment that night, and she quietly walked in.

"You live here, Gerald?" She asked, looking around the small apartment.

Only her bra and panties covered her. Her black dress was in my hand. I didn't wish to stop my hand from being in contact with what heavenly belonged to it. She had preserved the fair whiteness of her skin over the years, and though she looked paler, she was still my fair goddess.

"Yes." I smiled and gently squeezed my hand around her dress.

The half-naked figure of this pretty girl that would have aroused devils in me in earlier times now stirred nothing but something uniquely passionate that moved inside the cage of my chest. I just stood and watched her. She walked to the only window in the room and pulled back the curtain. It was dark outside except for one lamppost whose lower body was covered with posters. After a short while she pulled the curtain back and sat on the edge of my bed. She laid her arms on her knees and lowered her head and her silky hair covered her face. The happy expression on my face started to vanish on hearing her quiet weeping. I approached her and sat next to her.

"What's wrong with me, Gerald?"

I shyly put my hand around her shoulder.

"Nothing is wrong with you. You are as perfect as ever." I kissed her head, and the smell of her hair indicated that it had been unwashed for a couple of days or that her scalp had sweated heavily. "But we do need to talk about things."

"Talk about what?" Her voice was quiet and slow.

"Nothing special."

She put her head on my chest, and her wet cheek dampened my T-shirt and the skin underneath.

"I missed you so much. I . . . missed you," she said.

My hand stroked her hair, and after a while I could hear the sound of her breathing. She must have been tired, I guessed. My hand was in direct contact with her fresh skin, and my nose sniffed through her hair. Nothing existed around me but her, and no earthly perfume was capable of stirring me more than her body odour, warm and undiluted. The chemistry of perfumery was disguised in her; unreal things become so real under the influence of love. I felt no guilt about my past; my presence with Fang was my present, I believed. A promise of true death-defying happiness arose in the top of my heart.

My eyes fell on her thighs, her flat belly, and her small cleavage—my angel in my arms. I picked up a small blanket with one hand and pulled it over her and then laid her head gently on the pillow. I carried the only chair in the room and set it up next to the bed. I brought my drawing tools; she was to be the subject of the picture.

My eyes were opened by a small noise. I found myself on the chair. The sky outside was lit by early aurora, and the dim light coming through the window on my side didn't help my blurred eyes locate Fang on the bed. I rubbed my eyes and looked left, and there she was scanning through my collection of books one by one and throwing them aside.

"What are you doing?" I smiled.

I was expecting some sort of joke from her, but she jumped in alarm at the question and her eyes widened.

"Who are you?" she screamed and then covered her chest with a big book of Shakespeare's plays. "What have you done with me?"

It was a terrible nightmare hearing those words from her. I could see it wasn't a joke, because her face carried a really hard expression. I took the drawing pad and pencil from my lap and put them on the bed. I left the chair and started to take some paces towards her, when her sharp voice stopped me.

"Stop where you are. Stop or . . ." She picked up a thick book now, Dickens's *David Copperfield*.

"I am not going to hurt you."

I raised my hands open and held them at shoulder level. She calmed down a little and lowered the thick book in her hand, but nonetheless she was in defensive mode. I approached her slowly, and she swallowed hard as if waiting to see what would come out of the wild animal in me.

"Gerald, I am Gerald." I said, but the wondering look on her face was starting to worry me.

"I don't know you . . ." Tears were gathering in her eyes. "Please don't hurt me."

With the fall of her first tear drop, my heart ached. Things seemed to be a bit scary, and I could feel that something was wrong. I found my heart wishing that everything was in order.

I calmly sat next to her on the floor. The dust of the floor covered my palms as I laid them there. Fang's pretty face was veiled with thick melancholy.

"Gerald," her nose was wet when she sniffed.

I slowly moved my arm around her and laid it on top of her shoulder. She trembled and then felt more relaxed. I pushed her head towards me under my chin. My thick beard scratched against her thin hair.

"Gerald," she retorted.

"I am here . . . with you forever." I kissed her head.

"Where have you been for all these years?" She brushed her nose with one finger. "What is wrong with me? I was grieved beyond everything by you." She circled her hands around my waist tightly. "You left me behind when you left, and I lost myself without you."

"I am sorry for everything I have done and for the bad person I am." Tears poured down my cheeks. "I love you," I said in a whisper.

"Promise me not to part from me again." She planted a kiss against my sweating chest, whose temperature increased with the warmth of her body.

"I promise . . . till death does us apart."

Once a glimpse of life started to ripen in the soil of my heart, a monstrous worm grew and started to eat all the crops. I cannot imagine how a man could live with all the pieces of his soul blown apart, seeing that life would no longer entice a single wave of glee within his heart. I noticed that Fang suffered memory loss to an abnormal extent. She would share talks and laughter with me for hours and then cease to know me all of sudden, as if we haven't met before. I had to write everything on a board and in notebooks for her so as to remind her of her and me. It seems that she would forget everything during the hours of memory shutdown except for my name. Her mouth ritually repeated my name.

I did some research about her symptoms, and I came across dementia and Alzheimer's. Yes, it is true that Fang suffers anxiety and depression as I noticed, but she is so young for such a disease. I took her to a couple of hospitals, and they all confirmed that whatever she was going through is nothing sophisticated; it might be related to some family inheritance or just anxiety because of another disease she carries. I don't know about medication, and I cannot tell whether the doctors I have seen know anything about the symptoms of memory loss; I cannot contradict what I don't know. But alas, as if one sort of punishment isn't enough, Fang has been diagnosed with HIV as well.

I have never been so glad to stay close to anybody as I am with Fang, though our closeness has never been filled with big smiles and loving kisses. Tiny particles of mirth were all we shared even at the time of her wellbeing with her memories. We kissed and hugged but never had sex. My lust and craving for sex vanished in a cloud of pure love. Being with her became my ultimate goal. She would become violent at times and hammer me with books or whatever she might lay her hands on; once she injured my hand with a knife she had hid under the pillow.

I would disguise myself as her brother at times when she is not in her right mind, and I would give her a bath; she would be my sick sister. She has told me many versions of stories about her life and the things she encountered since the day we separated. I couldn't pick any one of them as the simple truth.

Almost four months have passed now since I met Fang again. I rented a small cottage on top of a mountain to stay in tranquillity with her, my dear obsession. The air is always gentle here, and it brings quiet refreshment to Fang; she seems quieter even in her periods of madness. It is here that I completed my book, *The Way to Suicide*, and one day upon reading a few lines from it, Fang asked me whether I am planning to encourage suicide among people. I gave no answer.

But the question of why we are not allowed to commit suicide has haunted me. Aren't we free to choose our lives and to seek the best path? What if you are in a dark tunnel and see nothing at the end of it but darkness? How long will you seek light when there is no light? How long will you seek refuge from tyranny when your land is forever occupied? The one common thing in life is sorrow. We may struggle and fight against it, but it will always seek us out. It requires quite an effort to get busy living, but it takes only a single moment of honesty with your own self to calm your alarm about death. Death is the ultimate end and the only truth about the fascinating nicely narrated fairy tales of life. Life's justice is injustice in the sense that all the false jewels are disguised under the promising, eye-tricking image of diamonds. Do you see life as just when there are people like me, with all the mental ability to achieve anything in life and yet striving for some unattained happiness, while there are others who are fascinated and in love with life, who would struggle to attain a single skill but still fail to do so? Would it not be right if my intelligence had been given to that hard-working guy who would use it to its full extent to bring something useful to life, while I was left with that man's poor mind to die on the side-lines of life?

People may look at suicide as a sign of weakness and lack of will. They ignore the fact that it is one of the choices people might take under circumstances in which, if those critics were dropped in, they would follow the same path that is followed by those they criticize. Suicide represents the freedom to control our life the way we see fit. It is not, it seems, about some enticement; it is a conscious choice of healthy sanity. Rebels we were born, and we shall keep that flame alive. We shall say what we believe we need to say, and we shall die as we choose to die.

When you read a story and get attached to a character in it, you just wish to see that character win and be victorious at the end of the story, but not every character's end tends to please us. For me, the end of Jude Fawley in *Jude the Obscure* was irritating and outrageous, but seeing it from the other point of view, it was the best the author Thomas Hardy could have done with him, and to expect any other end for such a fighter in life would have stolen the whole integrity of his character. Jude's death dignified the agony of his life. Werther is a fascinating character in *The Sorrows of Young Werther*, but he, in a heart-breaking scene, decides to take his own life. Werther demonstrated the truth of the fact that when you really feel life, you feel its pains. It is the honesty of the character that created a loud resonance among those who felt him. The problem with some people is that they like to just throw empty criticism and judgments that add nothing to the fact that suicide is just an end like any other form of death. Aren't brave soldiers encouraged to go to wars, knowing in advance they will be slaughtered, as long as the combat is for a sacred principle? Shall we consider those soldiers weak and negatively sensitive? If we see and believe that we are a burden on life, if we are no longer needed in life, if we seek and fail to find a longer-lasting beam of encouragement to cling to life, shall we not seek for our weeping suffering souls a shelter that may provide eternal peace?

They say that in life there are two kinds of people, sinners and saints, but that all depends on the way we perceive it. One may be treated as a saint while committing sins with full consent, while others may be looked at as sinners while adding only good deeds to life's narrow basket. Some criminals may believe themselves to be messengers of God, while others woven into society and buried in temples may see themselves as no better than any mere sinner. Well, "saint" is a useless word when spoken of someone on earth in order to justify some of the sins we commit when comparing our deeds with those we embrace as saints. Saints should be the foundation on which to judge our behaviour. There are no saints here. We are all just damned sinners. We are nothing but shadows and dust. A simple farmer committing suicide is no more a sinner than a priest, dressed in a godlike dress to conceal his true image.

I am now reaching the end of this story that I have been working on for the past month. My day has come. I don't know what I have left behind or if there is anything worth tracing. Fang is so cute when asleep; my heart throbs just looking at her. I would make her all the origami shapes I have mastered, and they would bring her temporary happiness. I would play guitar for her, and she would dance for me.

Last night she asked me when we are going to get married. It is the question with no answer, and the guilt of a lie would be so heavy if I promised her anything in this regard. I gave her my word that I am not going to leave her again. It is an oath that I am not going to break. I will be taking her with me and saving her from abandonment and the cruelty of life.

It is five minutes to five in the morning. The first arrows of the sunlight have started to rise. A fresh tickling air just announced its visit through the small open window in front of me, spreading inside the stony perfume of the mountains. Yesterday night I dressed Fang in a new dress that I purchased, a long sleeveless dark green, and I am dressed up now in simple full black. In a couple of minutes, I will be taking Fang with me off the cliff that started growing some green plants last week. It may be a painful way to die, but it is what I have chosen. It may look so unromantic, but I don't seek any romanticism in death. I am leaving this book on the table. Remember that this book isn't meant to send any hidden message. It is mainly the story of my life, in which all the pearls have been mixed with tears.

Adieu pain . . .

.

Also by the same author:
Secret Feelings published by Dorrance Publishing Company, US.

About the Author

Abdulla Kazim is a native of the United Arab Emirates. He holds a bachelor's degree in Business Information Technology from Dubai Men's College. Currently he is living with his wife and child in Dubai and works as a programmer in Dubai Aluminium Company.